GRAND RISING

WRITTEN By: TYEMEASE

CHAPTER 1

"You ready bro," G-Rock asked as he pulled the Grey Honda Accord over?

"Definitely," Row responded as he reached in the back seat and grabbed the bag of what would usually be filled with money when they made moves like this but today that wasn't the case. This time wasn't anything in it but newspapers and books.

"Sit behind Charlie and I'ma sit behind the fat goofy dude," G-Rock ordered.

Row nodded his head in agreement but he was getting more and more nervous by the second.

"When I tell you to give him the bag that's when we going to make it happen. Until then just chill regular. You know he be trying to hold conversations like we really friends, so just talk or whatever."

G-Rock pulled behind the Silver Maxima with their two Dominican friends in there who they had been buying coke off of for years now. They both got out of the car and into the back seat of the Maxima.

"Que pasa mi amigos," Charlie said greeting his friends. Charlie always seemed high in spirits when meeting with Row and G-Rock. Probably because he knew that it was a lot of money about to come his way. Money has a way of making people feel jolly.

The driver never said much. He was just an escort and shooter. Even though he looked like he wasn't killing anything other than Bologna Sandwiches. He always sat there with a dumb smile on his face nodding his head yeah every time Charlie said something no matter what he said. He exemplified a true yes man.

They started talking about the usual, how was family and business going. "G-Rock, what you plan on doing with that laundry mat you got on 7th street," Charlie asked while looking back at G-Rock?

"I'm thinking about turning it into an auto body shop," G-Rock said.

"That's good money, laundry mats only bring in change. You need something that's going to bring in dollars."

"I hear you. Everything add up but you got something else in mind?"

"We're going to have to get together and talk about that. You have to think about a used car dealership," Charlie said turning to look back at G-Rock again.

"That's a good idea," G-Rock said. "I'll keep that in mind." G-Rock tapped Row and told him to give Charlie the bag. Row passed the gym bag through the two seats. Charlie who was in the passenger seat took the bag and sat it in his lap and kept talking. After dealing with each other so long the trust level was high. It had to be when trusting someone with a couple hundred thousand dollars of any product, but Charlie seem to have forgotten that aint no honor amongst thieves and that the line of work they were in wasn't a trustworthy business.

Charlie was still talking when Row pulled the gun out from under his jacket and pressed it to the back of the seat and started shooting. The desert eagle at close range cut Charlie's sentences short. G-Rock shot the driver in the head, back, and upper neck finishing him immediately. His brains were panted on the

4

windshield and his face was pressed on the steering wheel. He was lifeless but his eyes were open and he seem to be looking at Charlie who somehow made it out of the car.

The passenger car door was open, Charlie was on his hands and knees trying to crawl away. Row had gotten out on his side of the car. He couldn't understand how Charlie could take so many shots and still be moving. What Row didn't know was that Charlie had a vest on. Maybe the trust level wasn't what it appeared to be after all.

"Get that mothafucka," G-Rock yelled to Row. He already bodied the driver so when he seen Charlie get out the car he got out and ran around to the front of the car to cut him off.

Row walked up behind Charlie while he was trying to crawl away like a dog. He kicked him in the ass and flatted him out on his stomach. Charlie rolled over.

"No no my friend, I'll give you whatever. Millions right now," Charlie said in his deep Spanish accent pleading for his life.

"Shut ya bitch ass up and die with some dignity." Row stood over him and gave him three shots to the face. They popped the trunk of the Maxima, took out the bags of coke and jumped in their car and left.

GRAND RISING

CHAPTER 2

"Pass the ball, let me get that," J-Mill yelled to Rek. He had Pooh in the low post. As soon as Rek passed him the ball he fake left made a move to his right and laid the basketball up.

"That's game," J-Mill said Nodding his head up and down knowing he just shitted on Pooh.

"Run that back," Pooh said holding the ball in between his right arm and hip. It was late night but the Campbell Soup night lights brightened up the basketball courts.

"You alright but you aint Tim Duncan," Fly said talking trash.

"I'll shit on the whole downtown. Who you want to put ya money on?"

"You crazy," Fly said getting the ball from Pooh and dribbling it. Fly was a high yellow light skin dude who was mixed with black and Puerto Rican. Usually he a be on the chubby side but he smoked so much weed that his weight was down. He was from downtown but ran a set near Campbell Soup for Meek who was from Parkside. Meek was one of the biggest drug dealers in the city.

"I'm thirsty," Taj said.

"The pizza store still open around the corner," Fly said.

"Ya treat," J-Mills asked joking?

"Come on, I got ya'll."

Fly and J-Mills had been friends for a long time. Even though fly was older than J-Mills by about 3 years and they were from different parts of the hood it has always been a friendly vibe between them. They got to the store and Fly pulled out a stack of

6

cash and paid for all of their food. J-Mills knew Fly was getting to it but seeing it had him envisioning himself with money like that. It never dawn on him that most of that money wasn't Fly's. Because he ran the block he collected money every couple of hours so his pockets stayed fat. They stayed in the pizza store for a while, ate and talked while taking turns playing the pinball ball machine.

"We out bro, be safe out here," J-Mills told Fly.

"You don't get no safer than this," Fly responded as he lifted the right side of his shirt up revealing a Glock 9.

"That thing look real good on ya hip, just make sure you bust it when it's time," J-Mills said laughing.

Fly faked a right jab at him making J-Mills flinch. They always played or had some type of jokes for one another.

"I would of dipped that slow shit. Yo, tell Tracy I sent my love too," J-Mills said talking about Fly's sister.

"Fuck outta here," Fly shot back before walking back to the block.

When J-Mills and his boys got to Rek house Bad was out front waiting for Rek. When they got on the porch Bad and Rek begin splitting up some money. They would put their money together buy some coke and trap it on Louis and Chestnut. Mainly Bad, Rek who was a little younger would trap sometimes but most of the times he would be with J-Mills smoking, playing basketball or trying to get with some chicks.

That night they all stayed over Rek's house. Typical young boy stuff, they watched YouTube videos and played games. Duheem who was Rek's older brother was already into the streets.

He had J-Mills ear and was telling him about the coke he just flipped. He trapped around on Louis and Chestnut also.

"It's easy," he said. "If you got good work and ya bags nice they going to want yours. They do anything for this shit, I be having the aunties sucking me off and everything. Dudes we grew up with moms," Duheem boasted. They both started laughing because of how Duheem said it.

"I been telling Rek for a minute to see what's up with B.O.."

"Fuck that," Duheem said cutting J-Mills off. "I'll give you something to trap tomorrow, I got you."

He had J-Mills thinking that he was really doing his thing. J-Mills didn't know any better, he didn't know anything about the game. All he knew was that if Duheem was in a position to give him something to trap then he must was doing something.

Tomorrow couldn't come fast enough. When J-Mills woke up Duheem was already gone. Figuring that he was already on the block J-Mills went home for a while. Later that day he went around Louis and Chestnut looking for Duheem but couldn't find him. Just him asking a couple of dudes where he was brought up the discussion of Duheem messing some money up. Come to find out on the block he was known as a gut artist. One of them dudes who always ended up messing up money no matter who they got work from. Dudes on the block joked about it and ran through different scenarios like they were flashbacks of a comedy show. Meanwhile J-Mills was disappointed. Today was supposed to be his big day. The day he had been waiting on for some time.

A couple of days later J-Mills and Pooh was walking down Park Boulevard going towards the Ave (Haddon Ave) when they seen people running towards some action. They followed suit, running around there to see what was going on. When they got there they seen Smoke who was the latest dude who Duheem had owned money to beating Duheem up. Slamming him on top of cars, punching him in his face, straight young boying him. Duheem tried fighting back but Smoke was older, bigger and drunk with the rams.

"You lucky, if you was somebody else I would of killed ya little ass," Smoke said then smacked the shit out of Duheem one last time. The whole time Smoke was beating him up he was talking to him.

J-Mills and Pooh stood there and watched Duheem get ragged. They could of rolled Smoke out and won but they didn't want to get in the middle of something so serious when it was something that Duheem did on the regular and on purpose. Money was the motive behind a lot of dudes in Camden death. When compared to that an ass whooping wasn't that bad.

Rek came out of nowhere and grabbed Smoke off his brother and Smoke started going on him. That's when everybody began breaking it up. J-Mills and Pooh was going to ride with Rek no matter what. Later they found out that Duheem had got Smoke for two ounces. Not that J-Mills was a pussy but after that day he vowed that when he got on that he wasn't going to be a fuck up.

CHAPTER 3

J-Mills walked out of the Bodega (Spanish store) on Princess and Wildwood and took an overview of the seen. It was a typical day in CMD (Camden). The chickens were out with their short shorts on flirting with the drug dealers. One guy was getting his car washed while another had his system loud playing Lil Durk. The fiends were lined up to cop their drugs. This was the hood. As fucked up as it may seem from the outside looking in it's nothing like it. It gave a lot of pain but it also gave pleasure that can't be duplicated in any other part of society.

Besides wanting to be a football player J-Mills also always wanted to be a drug dealer. It wasn't the glitz and glamour of the drug game that attracted him more than it was the money, power and the freedom to do what he wanted when he wanted the most. He knew early in life that money was the solution to all problems, and if one possess it, he or she could get people to do whatever one wanted them to do.

Beep Beep, a car pulled up in front of J-Mills taking him out of his thoughts.

"Get in," a voice said.

J-Mills looked in the car and saw his manz Mir. He was driving a Grey Chrysler 300. No doubt J-Mills knew it was stolen but with haste he jumped in the passenger seat.

"Where you get this from," J-Mills asked?

"Come on now with all these questions. Here roll this up," Mir said handing him a Dutch then pulling off. "You got money on you?"

"Yeah, why?"

"I'm about to go around Louis and Chestnut to buy some breakdowns. (A breakdown is a big bag of crack that one can buy and breakdown to make more than one bag out of it.)

"Where you going to trap (sell) them at?"

"Right there, who going to stop me," Mir said as if he could do what he wanted around there which wasn't the case?

They had a few dudes who trapped around there but it was B.O.'s block. Everybody around there got their work from him. J-Mills had been trying to get Rek to talk to B.O. about putting him on for the longest but Rek kept bullshitting telling him to talk to him his self. At the time J-Mills didn't feel like he knew B.O. good enough to be talking about that subject. At the same time he knew that all Rek had to do was put the word in and he was in.

"Let us get two," Mir said. Bad, Duheem, and Rek was sitting on an abandon house steps when they walked up.

"Dam, ya'll getting high now? Ya'll young as hell," Duheem joked.

"Nah, we about to trick Ms. Jones with these bags," Mir shot back referring to Duheem's mother. Dudes started laughing, Duheem became livid like he wanted to fight.

"Alright, remember you said that so you won't get mad when I try to hit ya old ass mom. You know she lonely as hell," Duheem said trying to get the last word.

"Ya'll bugging, let me get that money," Rek said as he handed Mir the bags.

After getting the bags they went in the old burnt up abandon store called The Silver Gallon and broke the bags down. After selling them they turned five dollars into twenty dollars and then did it again, this time buying more break downs. To J-Mills this was easy, free money, like taking candy from a baby. Automatically he started thinking long term. Mir's family had money. His mother was into real estate and his father worked for the state. They were divorced but still he was one of them dudes who wasn't broke in the hood. He did things because he could.

They were all in Silver Gallons trapping. Fiends knew if they didn't see them on the block than more than likely they were in there. B.O. came in and went straight to the back with this thick ass Puerto Rican chick. They could still see them but nobody really paid them any mind except J-Mills. B.O. whipped out, the chick got on her knees and started giving him head.

"Who that," J-Mills asked Rek in a low tone?

"That's Ria," Rek responded. He already knew what was on J-Mills mind. Ria was a beauty that somehow got strung out. She was in the early stages of smoking crack so she still looked good. "Chill, you going to get ya turn. She smoke," Rek told J-Mills.

"She smoke," he asked shocked? "Dam, she nice. I'm trying to hit that," J-Mills said grabbing his pants adjusting his manhood. "What's up Auntie, how many," he asked turning towards another fiend?

"Let me get four baby," The crackhead lady who had walked up said smiling with only about two pieces of furniture left in her mouth.

J-Mills dropped four bags in her hand and she looked at them disappointed.

"What happened to them big bags ya'll had last time," Auntie asked looking at Rek who must have served her last time?

"We going to have them later tonight," he responded.

The fiend left disappointed. B.O. came from the back and told Rek to give him two bags so he could give to Ria. J-Mills watched Ria's movement from the time she got the bags to when she was about to leave. Before she left she looked back and caught him staring at her butt. She gave him a wink, a smirk and shook her ass a little harder on her way out the door just for his entertainment.

"Ya'll got J-Mills out here, where you get coke from?" B.O. had just got the life sucked out of him and seemed to be in a good mood.

"I brought breakdowns," J-Mills said.

"Let me see em," B.O. asked? B.O. was putting out big bags to get the block banging. Them breaking the bags down and selling them on the same block was going against everything that he was trying to achieve. Once he seen how little they were he knew he had to nip that in a bud.

"Ya'll killing the flow with this little shit. If ya'll want work just let me know but I can't allow this. I'ma let ya'll finish whatever ya'll got today but after that if ya'll trying to trap out here it gotta come from me."

From the door Mir wasn't beat. He said that he was good. He felt like if he was going to sell drugs then it was going to be for himself. Every hustler has to start somewhere though. For J-Mills that was the door he had been waiting for to open. He was tired of being broke. His gear wasn't like the rest of the dudes he hung around. The only reason his dudes aint clown him was because he was nice with his hands. He didn't care to know what they were saying behind his back.

"I'm wit it. When do I start?"

"I'ma have something for you tomorrow," B.O. said.

J-Mills left that night with a little over a hundred dollars in his pockets feeling better than he ever did before. For him this was life changing, a dream come true type stuff. He knew his friends couldn't possibly understand what was really going on. To him they were going to a gold mine every day and was taking it lightly.

That night he went home to what was basically a crack house. (A crack house is a crib where fiends go to get high at. They pay the host who in this case is his mom a portion of what they're smoking to get high there.) The house had a permanent crack smell. He walked in and seen a woman he'd never seen before sitting on his couch smoking a pipe. She took a blast then looked at him like he was in the wrong spot.

"I gotta get the fuck outta here," he mumbled to himself.

He walked up the stairs and seen his mother through the half crack door, then he seen a man. His mother shut the door when she seen it was him. J-Mills knew she was in there tricking and getting high. He hated his living conditions and resented his mother for having him living like that. It's been going on for so long that he became immune to it all.

J-Mills never knew his father. For all he knew his pop could have been one of them Johns his mom was tricking off with. For J-Mills selling drugs wasn't an option, it was a choice he needed to make to support himself. Going to school looking dirty wasn't cool, especially where he was from. On holidays growing up he always felt some type of way hearing his boys always talking about the things they got or the experiences they had. He never had a real family, only a renegade mother who drug him along through life as she got high. As far as he could remember she got high. She spent her life chasing crack and forgetting about her only son.

He unlocked the lock on his room door and went in. This was his sanctuary. The only place in the house he felt safe. He didn't have a T.V. so he used his phone and listened to and watched YouTube videos. He zoned out, the whole time thinking about going out the next day getting to that money.

CHAPTER 4

Over the next few months J-Mills hugged the block faithfully. Money was his motivation so everything revolved around the block. He started having new clothes on the regular and was now attracting more females.

Summer was over and school was in. School wasn't really J-Mills or any of his friends strong suit but going to Camden High was like going to the club. Dudes was in there high, fly, and pushing up on every chick moving. This day on the way to school it was J-Mills, Mir, Rek, Pooh, Wez, and Duheem. Duheem was rolling up a wet blunt on the low. Neither J-Mills nor Mir smoked wet. Duheem knew this but being the slimy dude he was he sparked it, took a couple of pulls and passed it to Mir. Mir wasn't paying him any attention when he was rolling up. The thought of him putting wet in the dutch never crossed his mind, he started smoking and kept talking shit how he usually did.

"Fuck you roll half a jar," Mir asked because of how short and skinny the dutch was? All along he kept taking pulls. "This some dirt, where you get this from? Why this shit smell funny?" Mir smelt the tip of the dutch then looked at it with a scrunched up face then he looked at Duheem for confirmation.

Pooh and Duheem couldn't hold it in any longer. They burst out laughing. Knowing that they were the only two who smoked wet out of all of them confirmed his current thoughts.

"This wet aint it," he asked looking at them with the stupid face?

While they were still laughing at him he threw the dutch at Duheem's face and hooked off punching him in the head. They

16

started fighting, Pooh picked up the dutch and began smoking it. This was nothing new, them two stayed going at it over something. After they got tired and started holding each other everybody broke it up. Mir felt like he had won so he kept talking trash.

They got to school late. Pooh, Wez, and J-Mills was in the same class. As soon as they walked in Ms. James knew they were high. She kicked them out of her class sending them to the nurse where they were supposed to get urine tested. Something that wasn't new to them but instead of going to the nurse they left school and went around the corner on Orman to their friend's Reef house. Reef had already dropped out of school. His parents worked all day so they were never home. His crib was where they would bring their chicks and smoke weed during school hours. Once in the house Pooh went straight to the fridge like it was his house..

"I had a feeling ya'll was going to show up," Reef said like he was expecting them. "I got some haze in my room."

J-Mills went right upstairs to get that. Reef didn't tell him about the other thing he had in his room. Cookie was a chick they had plenty of times. She was in there under the covers watching videos. Wez came in the room right after J-Mills. Reef must have told him that she was up there. She was all smiles when they came in. She knew they were going to want some and she was with it. J-Mills sat on the edge of the bed and peeled the covers back revealing her petite frame.

"It's cold," she whined as she pulled the covers back over her body. She only had a thong on. When J-Mills seen her body he got rocked up.

"How bout I get under there with you to keep you warm," J-Mills suggested.

"Come on," she responded.

Cookie was a cutie. Light skin, long hair, green eyes with a nice body. Anybody who wasn't from Camden or who didn't know her would try to pursue her as their wifey but she was a true freak.

Pooh was downstairs eating cereal talking to Reef. When they came upstairs to the room they seen all asses. J-Mills was laying there while Cookie was sucking him off and Wez was hitting her from the back.

"Dam, why you aint tell me you had some pussy up here? You got these dudes hogging everything," Pooh told Reef as he started coming out of his clothes so he could get in on some of the action.

CHAPTER 5

G-Rock pulled across the street from the Camden County jail. Little Man made an exit and took a deep breath smelling the fresh air of freedom. "It's nothing like it," he said before he started bopping towards the gate with a big manila envelope full of his mail in it. After spending three and a half years in the county and beating a felony murder charge for carjacking and killing Dough Boy from the Hill he was Vampire Pale. G-Rock got out of his truck and embraced his bro. Even though they kept in touch over the phone they haven't seen each other in years. The only reason he was free today was because G-Rock and a couple other dudes had put some work in on a few witnesses.

"This what I'm talking about," Little Man said sizing the Navy Blue Range Rover up. It was freshly detailed sitting on black 24 inch rims.

"This how we doing it brah. Them pictures I was sending you was the real deal."

When Little Man left they were getting money but not how they are now. On top of that he wasn't focused so he didn't get the full thrill, plus he was on the run.

They got in the Range Rover and G-Rock shot over Philly. They blew a few stacks hitting about five different stores on south street. G-Rock wanted to make sure his dude was good before being seen in the hood.

"We going to throw something for you tonight. I rented the Buff Hall. You know the hood going to be in there heavy, plus chicks from all over. They was going crazy when I told them you was coming home, specially ya old thing Sonya."

"I aint fucking with her no more. She left me hanging. Take me to ma spot in Pine Hill."

****

A lot of people turned out to show Little man love at his home coming party. All the hard liquor drinks was free for everyone. The Champagne was for everybody who was in their section. It was two bouncers at the door checking everyone, the only dudes who had guns on them were dudes they delt with. The females outnumbered the men three to one. People from all over was there. The Party spilled over to the outside, one didn't have to be inside to be having a good time.

It didn't take much for Little Man to get nice since he hadn't had a drink in years. He was drinking Remy Martin 1738, that was his favorite drink. He stood there feeling drunk and free observing the seen thinking about how the turnout was for him. Through the crowd he peeped his manz Coon from downtown. He was on his way over there to see what was good with him when he was cut off by this chick he used to mess with.

"Hey Little Man, I miss you," Sonya said all drunk trying to hug on him.

She was a light skin cutie, about 5'5, shoulder length hair, a tight body with a nice fatty. She also had a lot of sex appeal and knew how to dress but Little Man was disgusted by the site of her. She must of thought because he was home that he was going to forget how she left him for dead. She thought he was finished because he was facing life in prison. Now that he was home she was back on his top. He expected that from a lot of people, that's how fake people moved.

Little Man didn't have to say anything his facial expression was saying it all. She was just either too drunk or dumb to read it. He was looking at her as though she stunk of a foul odor or was a decease that he wasn't trying to catch. She was blabbing about something when he took her face into the palm of his hands and mushed the shit out of her extra hard. "Fuck outta ma face," he said all in one motion. She went flying across the room and he continued to find his peoples he was supposed to be talking to.

Everybody was looking wondering what was going on. She got up angry trying to yell at him through the music but he disappeared in the crowd.

"I'ma get ma brother to fuck you up!"

Everybody was looking at her trying to figure out who she was talking to.

"You see this guy," G-Rock asked Tab as they watched Little Man and his antics? Tab is another member of G-Rocks squad, he had the set on Haddon.

"He back on his bullshit already," Tab said.

"Keep an eye on him," G-Rock told Tab before stepping off. Tab played the other side of the wall from where Little Man was at. He kept one eye on him and one on this chick that he had pulled to the side.

"Yo bro, what the hell happened over there," Coon asked laughing as him and Little Man shook hands?

They had did some time in the county together and was happy to see each other on the other side. They spoke for about ten minutes before a young lady had came over to Little Man and told him that G-Rock had wanted him outside. He didn't think twice. His manz wanted him he responded asap. He didn't think anything was suspicious. He excused himself from Coon and drunkenly walked towards the exit.

When he got outside G-Rock was nowhere to be found. He tried looking through the crowd of people but couldn't spot him. Meanwhile dude behind him was lifting his gun up to point it at Little Man but Tab who had followed Little Man outside seen everything before it happened and grabbed dude's arm, the gun went off as they tussled. At the same time everyone outside begin dispersing. Little Man turned around and started helping Tab. Another one of their men went over and started helping them. When the smoke cleared dude laid there beat up and shot twice with his own gun.

****

The next day they were in one of G-Rock's spots on Princess Ave. "You know that was dude manz that you bodied from the Hill," Row told Little Man. They were in the house smoking and watching the basketball game.

"I figure it had to be. If it wasn't for Tab he would of knocked ma shit off," Little Man said pulling on the dutch slightly smiling. "Now I'm going to give them all the rec they want."

"All that bullshit be having them fed boys on they shit, we trying to get money," G-Rock said.

"I feel you, you right. I'll handle that on some other type time. I'm trying to get money too, I aint trying to wait."

"Where you want in at," G-Rock asked Little Man?

"Louis and Chestnut and wherever else you make room for me at. You know once ma feet get wet I'ma start moving out."

"It's a bunch of young boys out there now," G-Rock told em.

"I know, I blew through there. The older dudes know who I am. Them young boys are going to fall right in place. They looking for guidance anyway."

"You can't be on that old head prison stuff with these young boys."

Little Man heard what G-Rock was saying but he wasn't really trying to hear him.

CHAPTER 6

When Little Man came home B.O. wasn't sure what type of time he was going to be on. Louis and Chestnut was originally Little Man's block but before he had gotten locked up he had fell off and word was that he was getting high on his own supply. He was B.O.'s old head but B.O. was hoping that he had other plans because all the money was coming back to him. He was a young old head amongst even younger dudes. When B.O. seen Little Man back with his squad he already knew what it was.

****

Duheem kept gutting dudes for their money. He'll spend his profit off the top and he wasn't one to hug the block for long so by him dipping off he wouldn't be making money so he'll also end up dipping into the money of whomever he had gotten the work from. Next thing that person would be looking for him for their bread.

The block was full of reckless young boys, it stayed hot with cops coming through there harassing them. Most of the young boys only sold drugs just to have a couple of dollars in their pockets. It was only a few who truly lived it and loved it, over time they would be the ones who'll rise to the top.

Little Man didn't come home like he was trying to take the whole block back, he just started putting work out there and since a couple of days ago B.O. ended up getting pulled over and locked up for some warrants J-Mills was the first to start getting work from Little Man. He was wondering why nobody else had done so especially since Little Man was also Rek's cousin.

"Rek, why you don't be getting anything from Little Man," J-Mills couldn't help but ask one day when they were on the block together?

"He be having some bullshit," Rek answered.

It was obvious Rek had better work because the fiends would request his more than J-Mills. These were things J-Mills would be picking up on as he learned the game. He thought it was because they knew Rek. He had been trapping since he was like ten. His whole family sold drugs, even his mom.

"He be fronting me ounces for the low," J-Mills said. He like the fact that he was getting ounces for under what they were going for and he was able to bag up and make the kind of money off of it he wanted while all his boys were only getting one twenty five or one thirty packs and had to bring back a hundred.

"That's why he giving it to you like that, because you moving that bullshit, but you be having to bag up extra fat and stay out here all long."

Little man had started J-Mills off with an ounce, but once he seen how fast J-Mills moved it and seen how trustworthy he was he kept giving him more and more.

"That's ma cousin but I aint selling that. Plus we got the same source now, and I'm getting fronted." Rek had started getting his work from G-Rock. The same source Little Man was getting his work from it's just when Little Man cooked up he stretched it to the limit to try to make as much as he could. As long as it was getting moved he didn't see a problem with it.

"He be giving you powder," J-Mills asked? He wanted to know, if so that would show that he moved up a level pass him. When they were dealing with B.O. they were all only getting packs.

"Yeah, I got ya uncle Red to cook it up for me and I put what I want on it," Rek said with a smirk trying to see if J-Mills was going to catch the joke he threw in there.

"Yeah alright, that's ya uncle." It was nothing slow about J-Mills. He just was new to the drug game. Even though it was always around him and in his house. Beside looking up to the guys in the game because they had nice cars jewelry and women he never understood how things really worked. One thing he knew was that one day he'll be involved.

Little Man was stretching his coke to the max. It wouldn't even rock up. At first J-Mills didn't know any better, he thought that was regular but hearing everybody else talking he began catching on. At first It really didn't bother him, the prices he was getting it for left him a good profit. That's all he cared about. He was young and getting money, and to him the getting money part was the only part that counted.

J-Mills loved the block, he was out there religiously. He wasn't like the rest, get a couple of dollars in his pockets and leave the block. During the summer he would break night on the regular trying to get his money right. Sometimes he would cut school and go to the block. Whoever he got work from he would bring them back straight paper. He had plans on being more than just a trapper. He had plans on running things one day, having dudes out there trapping for him, but right now he was just trying to soak up as much game as possible.

He brought his first car for two hundred and fifty dollars. For him that was big. The only car him and his boys were used to driving in was stolen cars. Now he had something he didn't have to run from the cops in. His dirty days were over. He kept dealing with

Little Man not because he was loyal but because his options was limited. Leveling up was always at the forefront of his mind though.

This day he had left Rek house and had went to the block. He was the only one out there so he chilled in The Gallon. How the Gallon was whoever was in there could easily see out but it was hard to see in. Ria came through looking for something.

"You got something," she asked?

"Of course," he responded unlocking the gate. She came in and they went to the back. He gave her two bags and she started sucking him. Her head game was whack so he put on a condom and started hitting it from the back. After he got off he couldn't help but to think *dam why this pretty chick out here selling herself short like this.* But all he could say to her was, "crack must be good, huh?"

"Best high ever," she replied. "You wonna try some?"

"Nah, I'm good."

On her way out she looked back at him and caught him staring at her again but this time it wasn't in lust.

"What are you doing coming out of the Gallon Ria," Taj asked? Sometimes they kept their stashes in there, he wanted to make sure she wasn't trying to steal.

"J-Mills is back there."

A moment later J-Mills came walking out, Taj started joking on him from the door. "That's all you do is trick."

"Man, you the trick master. You can't say nothing about me."

They went across the street to Sha who was sitting on the steps smoking. They were over there for about five minutes when Taj said, "pass the dutch deep throat. You necking shit."

"Yeah you had that thing for a minute," J-Mills added.

"I forgot I had this thing," Sha lied with the slow highed up look on his face. The whole time he was trying to keep the conversation going so they wouldn't realize that he was necking the haze.

"You aint forget to put that thing to ya lips though. Give me that shit," Taj said snatching the dutch from Sha.

Sha aint pay him no mind. Taj was animated. They were always doing things for laughs. Instead he turned around and started messing with J-Mills. "Ayo here come ya shorty," he said referring to Isha who was always coming through the block for J-Mills. "She stay on ya heels."

"At least I got something coming through. You starting to look suspect. You don't even be tricking any of the aunties coming through." Taj started laughing, Sha didn't respond. He really wasn't on no funny type time he just didn't get ass like that.

J-Mill, Taj, and Sha was on the step smoking when Isha and Monay walked up. J-Mill got up and greeted her with a hug and a kiss separating her from any of the other females he was dealing with. Isha was a brown skin beauty, about 5'4 a hundred and thirty pounds with a stuffy. She came out there on some lovely dovey stuff. She ended up taking out her camera and wanting to take pictures with J-Mills so she could post them and make all the other girls he was dealing with feel some type of way. All of them out there ended up taking pictures.

"I'm coming through tonight, like ten," J-Mills said grinding on her butt, still in the same position that they took their last picture in.

"I want you to come over earlier than that. Like 8:00 O'clock," she said being demanding.

J-Mills thought about it for a quick second then agreed. He had a weak spot for her. Even though he tried not to show it. They had been dealing with each other for about a year. From the door he noticed that she possessed some qualities that was rare in females nowadays. She was loyal, respected herself, and knew how to treat him that's why he didn't have a problem compromising with her.

"How ya'll getting home?"

"Monay Aunt taking us, she live on Kenwood," Isha responded.

"Alright, see you tonight." They hugged and the two ladies left.

"Yo, tell her to hook me up with one of her friends," Mir told J-Mills. The whole time they were out there Taj had been pushing up on her friend Monay.

"I'ma tell her. I got you bro, she got a lot of friends. They all nice too."

While they were talking Little Man pulled up in a Green Cadillac Truck. He had been doing his numbers since he been home. It was looking like he never left. J-Mills hoped in the passenger seat and they went to his house on Empire. Little Man gave J-Mills nine ounces, he took it in the house and came back out with the money he owed him from the other work.

"Next trip I wonna buy some raw. How much you going to charge me," J-Mills asked as they started riding? He could tell Little Man wasn't expecting to hear that question. He had a little shiesty smirk on his face, but he was really wondering what did J-Mills know about raw.

"How much you trying to buy?"

"Four and a half," J-Mills replied.

Little man was a little surprised. He knew J-Mills was different just by his hustle but he didn't know that he was smart enough to stack his money and progress in the game so fast.

"I'll sell it to you cooked up." He wanted to keep fronting him cook up so he could stretch it and make more money. It was the only reason he could afford to give it to him for the price he was giving it to him for.

"Nah, I want to put what I want on it. You be cutting it until it be all bake." J-Mills was starting to feel some type of way. He could tell that Little Man didn't want to sell him any powder. He was learning a lesson. That no matter how fly their relationship seemed to be that when it came to business nothing was personal. Little Man didn't really want to see him come up. He was only worried about his profit margin. J-Mills aint like when people tried to hold him down, he knew that he was going to have to stop dealing with him.

"I'm going to see what I can do," was what Little Man said when he dropped him back off.

****

That night J-Mills went to stay at Isha's place. She had her own apartment that she had moved into a couple months ago. She wanted J-Mills to come live with her because she knew his situation at home. He stayed there often and had clothes there but Westfield Garden was a little far from Parkside. Even though he told her he'll be there at eight it was about 9:30 when he finally arrived.

"I shouldn't have open the door for you," she said as she walked away after letting him in. She had a t-shirt on with some booty shorts. The bottom of her cheeks were hanging out of them.

"Why don't I got ma own key anyway?"

"Because every time I'm ready to give you one you act up and I decide not to."

"I lost track of time," he said walking behind her. She seemed to be mad because he didn't come at the time she wanted him to. She went in her room and shut the door behind her. Thinking it was funny J-Mills just smiled. He knew she could never stay mad at him for long. He opened the door and asked her did she cook.

"It's in the microwave," she said with an attitude not bothering to look up at him.

J-Mills went and ate. When he got done he went back to the room. She was still sitting up watching T.V.. He took his clothes off and got in bed. He started playing kissing on her lips, face, and neck. She was still sitting there with her arms folded acting like she was being unaffected but he knew all of her spots. He knew her pussy was getting wet. He could tell by the change in her breathing that he had her feeling good. He unfolded her arms and took her shirt off, then started kissing and sucking her breast. She started moaning, he got her to lay flat and was still licking and sucking on her. When he got back to kissing her lips she began kissing him back.

31

"I love you Jamil," she whispered as he kissed her neck. He slid down her booty shorts and took them off. He felt her pussy, it was soak and wet. He inserted a finger in her, he took it out and put it in his mouth for a taste. Then he went down and started licking and sucking on her clit. After about ten minutes of ecstasy she came, then he made love to her.

CHAPTER 7

J-Mills had went to Rek's house to bag up the work he had got from Little Man the night before. Rek had his scale out. Something had told J-Mills to weigh his coke before bagging it up. Ounce by ounce he placed them on the scale and they all said 25 grams. It was supposed to be 28. He kept checking, taking them down putting them back on there. He checked to see if the scale was calibrated right. Rek had put something on there and it came back right that's when J-Mills had to accept the fact that he was getting played.

"Yo this pussy been playing me," he said in disbelief. Instantly he became heated. His face was flushed.

"All of them was twenty five," Rek asked? J-Mills nodded his head. He didn't really want to talk. "Call em and tell em."

"Nah, he know what he was doing. This aint his first time getting me." J-Mills sat there looking at the coke contemplating his next move. All kinds of thoughts were going through his mind.

Rek was embarrassed because J-Mills was his manz and Little Man was his cousin. He knew the whole thing was wrong. This was one of the things he wanted to avoid, that's why he never brung J-Mills in when he asked. First he didn't want to be responsible if he gutted somebody for some money. On the flip side he also knew that the older dudes be taking advantage of the young boys lack of knowledge of the game.

"It's alright, I aint paying him shit. He going to have to take it in blood. Whatever is whatever," J-Mills said as if he wasn't sure he should be really saying it. Everybody in the hood knew that Little Man was a killer. He had just came home from beating two bodies

33

and J-Mills knew that but at the moment he was so mad that it didn't matter.

J-Mills started bagging up. His mind was set, he knew what he was going to do. He was bagging up and smoking Haze, coke on his fingertips and everything but he held the dutch between his fingers where there wasn't any coke.

"Your mom said come here right quick," Key Key told Rek.

J-Mills head popped up when he heard that voice.

"All she want is some money," Rek said before leaving the room.

"Dam Key Key where you been," J-Mills asked checking her out from head to toe? You looking good as usual, why I don't be seeing you like that anymore?"

"Because you don't ever call me," she responded.

She was Rek's cousin. A little light skin cutie with a nice butt. Her and J-Mills had sex a few times and always remained fly. Every time he ran into her he had to flirt and she loved it too.

"Want to taste this," he asked offering her the dutch?

"Boy, you know I don't smoke. Stop trying to drug me,"

"You know I don't need to drug you for you to get nasty. You know I know," he said smiling.

"I only do them things when I'm with you," she said.

"If I had a nickel for every time I heard that I wouldn't have to sell drugs." They both started laughing. They joked for a little then he ended up getting her to seal the baggies on the iron while he finished bagging up. He knew if he wanted he could of made her his girl but why mess up a good thing. He was able to have his way with her when he wanted. After they finished he promised to call her.

****

"Where everybody at," J-Mills asked as he walked up on Sha alone on the block?

"They at the telly with some chicks."

"Yeah, why you aint go?" J-Mills already knew the answer to his question. He just wanted to hear Sha's response.

"I gotta get this money."

J-Mills smirked and took his phone out, called Taj and told him that they were on their way. When they got to the room the chicks was in there loose, walking around naked. They had jointed rooms, hell of weed smoke and drinks. Snacks were everywhere and the beds looked like they had already missed an orgy. Reef was in the bathroom hitting one chick from the back with the door open for everyone else to see and hear. Pooh and another chick was on the bed smoking. The chicks was with whatever.

****

Every businessman knows their turnover rate. Same with the drug game, Little Man knew when J-Mills was supposed to be done the coke he had given him. Usually he'll get a call like clockwork but he didn't so he pulled up on the block wanting to get paid.

J-Mills had already flipped them nine ounces. When Little Man pull up he dipped into The Gallon and grabbed his 357 from under the steps and placed it on his hip. Little Man peeped him go in there and went in there after him.

"What's up little bro, you ready for me," he asked with that same sneaky smile on his face? He pulled out another nine ounces but could sense that something wasn't right because of how J-Mills was squared up and keeping his distance. They both heard a noise in the background. Little Man started looking around. J-Mills didn't bother he just responded to him.

"I aint paying you shit you slimy ass pussy."

That sneaky smirk Little Man always wore dropped right off his face and an angry one appeared. He didn't take disrespect kindly, especially not from young dudes. He reached for his gun but J-Mills had beat him to the draw and shot him four times in the chest. BOOM BOOM BOOM BOOM. Little Man hit the floor and curled up. J-Mill stood over top of him mean mugging thinking about putting one in his head but then decided not to. He could hear him grasping for air. He bent down and grabbed the coke out of Little Man's hand ran to the back up the stairs to the roof and made his getaway. He came out on Vermont street, ran through the alleyways all the way to the back of Forrest Hill School and threw the gun as far as he could in the Delaware River.

Dudes on the block heard the shots and knew they came from The Gallon but nobody went to see what happened. The police showed up about twenty minutes after the fact and found Little Man dead.

****

The whole time Rek was in The Gallon taking a piss when he heard somebody running in. He hid thinking it was the cops chasing somebody. Instead he seen J-Mills come in and grab his burner from under the steps, then he heard someone else come in. From where he was positioned he couldn't see who the other person was but he could hear them talking and it sounded like his cousin Little

Man. He tried to move to get a better view and as he did the box next to him made a noise so he stopped. Then he heard shots and seen J-Mills run to the back. He knew what just happened, he waited about a minute or two after J-Mills ran by because he didn't want him to know he was there. He knew the rules about not leaving any witnesses and even though J-Mills was his manz he wasn't trying to take any chances.

He came out and saw his big cousin laying there in a pool of blood. Little Man never bothered to look up as Rek stood there watching him take his last sips of air. Life was over for Little Man and Rek knew it. He was nervous and hurt because as much as he wanted to stay there he had to leave him. The police was going to need somebody to put the murder on and he didn't want it to be him. He knew they wasn't going to be trying to hear that cousin stuff. He got out of there through the back, the same way J-Mills had taken five minutes before.

When Rek made it home he couldn't stop playing the scene over in his head. His family had already gotten the news. News traveled faster than lightening in the hood. Not only did Rek witness the whole thing now he had to see his aunts and cousins crying. That hurt him the worse. While his family went to the crime scene he stayed home on the couch in a zone.

The next few days the block was hot. Nobody got any money out there. Homicide detectives was picking people up but wasn't nobody saying anything. That had them peeved. Every time something happened nobody would say anything. They was coming around the block so much it basically shut the block down. They eventually boarded Silver Gallon up.

CHAPTER 8

Everybody who trapped on Luis and Chestnut began migrating to different blocks. Most went to Haddon, some went on Princess while some went on wildwood. J-Mills didn't want to be on any of them spots. He finessed his way onto Liberty Street, the same block Pooh had went to. After a while Mir and Reef came up there too.

Liberty was a block that boarder Parkside and Pollock. At the time it was mainly a powder and weed flow, that dominated everything. The crack that was being sold out there was being sold by the dudes who sold weed and powder that's why it still was slow for that. Crack required a different type of hustle, and that's what J-Mills and his dudes brung when they went up there.

Everybody from the hood assumed they knew what happened to Little Man. All that just added to J-Mills reputation, but it was plenty of dudes walking around Camden with bodies under their belts so it was no big deal. Still the streets was talking and the police got ears and that made J-Mills nervous. Every time he saw vice, detectives or regular squad cars he thought they were coming for him. Even though the more time that went by the more he felt like he got away. It would always still linger in the back of his mind.

****

After about a month the heat begin to die down a little. Rek was in the back seat of G-Rock's Range Rover. They had just come back from a club over Philly. G-Rock and Row were the big men out Parkside. Since Rek was already getting coke from G-Rock when Louis and Chestnut got shut down he started being with them more.

"Word is ya boy J-Mills killed ya cousin," G-Rock said looking back at Rek.

"Fuck him, he aint ma manz," Rek responded with hostility in his voice. Ever since that day him and J-Mills haven't really spoken or seen much of each other. "He did kill him, I was there but he don't know it."

Should we get somebody to pay him a visit," Row asked looking at G-Rock?

The whole time G-Rock was thinking about what to do. If it was somebody from somewhere else that would of put Little Man down he would have been put the hit out but once he found out who J-Mills was related to he had to give him a pass.

"Nah, that's Melo nephew."

"I forgot all about that," Row said.

Even though his manz was gone apart of G-Rock liked that the young boys was putting in work. To him it meant that they were ready. "We going to pay him a visit, just not that kind. He might be of some value to us," G-Rock stated.

****

J-Mills woke up brushed his teeth, got in the shower and got dressed. Isha was acting like she didn't want him to leave. She was playing hiding his keys. He had been staying over there on the regular being as though that was where he kept his money and drugs. His mother had been breaking into his room pitching his stash. After playing with Isha, wrestling her down and taking his keys back they ended up having sex. Come to find out that was all she wanted. He put her to sleep then left.

****

39

Mir, J-Mills, Reef, and Pooh was out on Liberty Street on the side of Donkeys. J-Mills leaned against the wall with his leg up while his dudes stood around talking. A Royal Blue S 550 Benz slowly approached. The conversations stopped. They all knew who car it was but that thing was so pretty that all their heads were turning to admire it. It pulled over in front of them and G-Rock got out of the driver seat. Row was in the passenger seat. They could see Row smoking a dutch scrolling through his phone.

"J-Mills let me get a moment with you playa," G-Rock said. J-Mills reluctantly went, he was wondering what could he possibly want. They weren't completely strangers to one another. G-Rock was someone who J-Mills and his friends grew up idolizing. Plus he was friends with his Uncle Melo. At the same time he was also friends with Little Man and by now everybody was assuming that J-Mills was the one who did that to him.

"What's good," J-Mills asked trying to be confident as they shook hands? No matter what he wasn't about to coward to no man. He had this quietness about him that didn't allow people to read his thoughts. He was young but fearless, and emotionless.

G-Rock stood in front of the driver side door with his arms folded rubbing his chin. He was 6'1, dark skin, medium built with a closely cut beard and waves in his hair. J-Mills was light skin, with waves, just a light mustache, and a medium build also but to G-Rock he was just a young boy trying to come up.

"I heard you bust ya gun," G-Rock said smiling.

"You should too it's dangerous out here," J-Mills wittingly shot back now knowing where he was going with this conversation.

G-Rock like how sharp he was but then chose to get straight to the point. "I heard that was you who flipped Little Man. That was ya work?"

"I don't know what you talking about."

"Good answer. The problem with that is…" As soon as J-Mills heard problem he put his hands in his jacket and grabbed his trusted 9mm. G-Rock peeped his movement and told him to relax. He changed his tone and went into explanation mode. "What happened happened, I heard he was doing you wrong. Still he was a part of this PSM (Parkside Mob) thing. By losing him we lost a lot of money and truthfully the only reason we're having this conversation is because you're Melo's nephew. You know how close him and I were. I still keep in touch with him to make sure he don't want for anything."

J-Mills eased up but never took his hands out of his jacket. Now he was trying to figure out where G-Rock was going with this conversation. He wasn't getting money with them but he was from Parkside too. It was embedded in him, he stood on that and nobody could take that away from him.

G-Rock knew that about him. He seen him and his friends come up and knew their potential. He knew J-Mills was different, he seen how his friends treated him and spoke about him. One thing about a leader is that they have to have the ability to see further ahead than everybody else and G-Rock knew that he was staring at the future.

"I want you to join the Mob," G-Rock continued. "I like the way you move. You put in work and I can tell ya dudes follow ya moves."

J-Mills sat there listening to G-Rock big him up. He was flattered to hear this coming from someone he looked up to when he was younger. He was too thorough to show it though, he kept his poker face on showing no emotions or expressions. While G-Rock kept talking he occasionally nodded his head to let him know that he was paying attention.

"I'm Parkside all the way but what's going to be the difference?"

G-Rock smiled, put his hands in his pockets and leaned up against the car. He like how J-Mills was on it. Only real Parkside dudes had that Parkside Pride.

"I like that, but it's a difference," G-Rock said. "This the kind of shit you push when you really affiliated," he said referring to the Benz he was leaning on. "It's more than what you might think. Everything out Parkside that's moving no matter what it is comes through these hands." G-Rock flashed his hands in front of him as he talked. J-Mills heard what he was saying but he was a little dazzled by the pinky ring and bracelet that flashed before him. G-Rock was looking like he was on the set of a rap video.

"We come together for one major purpose and that's to get money. You pledge ya loyalty and you going to have access to all the coke you can move, plus guns and a lot of other benefits. You can take this little block over, have it banging in no time. Take ma number, I'ma let you think things through." J-Mills pulled out his phone and began to log G-Rock's number in. "I know you aint no dummy so I expect to hear from you by tomorrow. Be safe out here," G-Rock said and they shook hands.

G-Rock opened the door, looked at the other fellas who was out there and gave them a little head nod before driving off. The whole time they were over there speculating on what was being talked about. J-Mills came back over there and posted up. He knew his dudes was going to have questions.

"What he talking about bro," Mir asked?

J-Mills gave them the run down but left out the conversations about Little Man. He could tell they were getting excited, especially Mir. All he wanted to do was get money and shine. Nobody could knock him because he was a thorough dude.

"So what we going to do," Reef asked? He was all in on any decision J-Mills made.

J-Mills had already decided what he was going to do when G-Rock put the offer on the table. He just didn't want to give him the answer right then and there and seem thirsty. He knew if dudes detected any weakness then they'll exploit it.

That night J-Mills went home to Isha's house where he contemplated everything G-Rock had said. He thought he knew about everything that went on in his hood. He knew that certain dudes from certain blocks were fly with each other but not that they were all connected and that G-Rock and Row had the whole hood on smash. He knew they were heavy in the game and it was legendary in the hood how they put in work. Especially the one J-Mills heard about last years when they supposedly killed the two Spanish dudes at Camden High Park. Word was that they got them for fifty bricks of coke but nobody knew for sure what they came off with.

He also started thinking about all the other old heads Big Jamil and Reeve. Not only because they had the same name but also because of the way he moved. He really had Parkside on smash in his day. Big Jamil retired and became a fireman. He got all kinds of properties and stores in the hood. Then it was king who had True

Blue and the other old head Benny. Benny had caught an indictment with the organization. He had mansions and a yacht. These were guys who had inspire J-Mills when he was coming up.

J-Mills was laying in bed looking through his phone while Isha rested her head on his chest peacefully asleep. No doubt he was going to make that call. The only reason he was in the game was to get rich. Messing with G-Rock was looking like his mill ticket.

J-Mills called G-Rock to let him know that he was in but that he had to finish some other work first. At the time he was buying his coke from Coup and Plus. Two old heads from Lib. J-Mills, Mir, and Reef had become partners. They would put their money together and buy some work. Since Liberty wasn't an established crack cocaine flow yet it would take them a few days to finish what they had but they were dedicated to making it bang. They made it a twenty four hour flow, broke it up into shifts and slowly but surely with that Louis and Chestnut grind they brought up there the block started picking up.

When Pooh seen G-Rock approach J-Mills he wanted to be a part of what he knew was to come. He knew how them dudes was on it and he also knew that everybody who was in that circle got money. J-Mills and them didn't have any problems with Pooh coming on board. He was their manz. The only reason they was on Lib was because he opened that door for them.

CHAPTER 9

After the work they had was finally finished J-Mills and his partners decided to go to the liquor store on 7th and Chestnut. While riding down the Ave Taj had flagged them down. Ever since Louis and Chestnut had gotten shut down Taj had been hustling on the Ave for Tab. They pulled over and talked to Taj for a little then kept on route.

They pulled in front of the liquor store and called one of the fiends over to the car. Every hood had fiends that posted outside of the liquor store like it was their set.

"What's up nephew, what you need," the man asked as he came to the passenger side window? He dam near had his whole head in the car trying to see who was in the back seat.

"Smelly Melly," Mir yelled from the back seat.

"Back the fuck up," J-Mills told Mel.

Mel was smelling like water and soap was his worse enemies. He looked like he was living hell literally but when he saw them he flashed his rotten teeth knowing that he was about to make some money.

"Dam Mel, you everywhere."

"I gotta get ma hustle on nephew, you know how it is."

If Mel wasn't in front of that liquor store he had a cart with some cans or some other type of metal in it taking it to the junk yard for some money.

"I need you to get us a 5th of Henny, a six pack of Coronas and some cups. I got you when you come back."

Smelly Melly went in and came out with what they ordered. J-Mills gave him ten dollars and a Corona.

"Oh man, you always look out for me youngen. I'm ya guy when you come through."

They went to Reef house and J-Mills put his favorite mob movie on.

"How many times you going to have us watch this shit," Mir asked?

"You don't get it bro, you looking at it as another movie. That's us, you see how they put their thing together, that's what we have to do," J-Mills said trying to break the movie down so they could apply it to their lives. "You see how they chose who was going to be the face of their squad. They all played their parts to the fullest. That's how you get money. Lucky Luciano was the face, Maya was the brains, Bugsy Siegal was the muscle, and the other dude had the political and police connects on smash."

J-Mills talked through the whole movie breaking things down as it went along. They seen it as just another movie until he put it in different context for them. He was talking about trust, discipline, loyalty, and how real gangstas move. Pooh and Reef was really into what he was saying but Mir was one who always thought everything was sweet. The stuff he was talking they thought only existed in the movies. Political and Police connects was something foreign. To them if you was too friendly with the cops you must be snitching.

When the movie was over J-Mills cut the T.V. off stood up and said, "So how we going to do this? Tomorrow we getting a new connect. Ya'll know how they play. I don't know what he going to give us but he told me whatever we need it's there. I don't know about ya'll but I'm trying to get right. I been dreaming about this shit. The other dudes on Lib gotta go, if it aint coming through us it aint nothing. I aint playing with dudes. I'm trying to get real right and I need ya'll with me."

"I'm wit it," Pooh said.

"Me too," Reef added.

"Ya'll already know I'm with it," Mir added.

"Enough said."

So far everything was playing out how J-Mills wanted it to. They sat there talking about how they was going to put Lib on smash.

****

The next day G-Rock picked J-Mills up in his Range Rover. This was the first time J-Mills had been in one. He took in the feeling, how bossy it sat up, the plush leather seats. All this helped him set new standards for himself.

G-Rock was all business as they got on the Ben Franklin Bridge. He made it his business to lay down a couple laws, letting it be known that business was business, that he don't play with his money. J-Mills didn't take anything he said personal, he felt the same. Especially about not playing with his money. They went to Dwight's on Germantown Ave to get something to eat. They got their food and ate in the car. Afterwards they went back to their hood. G-Rock took him to Bradly Street and pulled behind a Tan Honda Accord. He gave J-Mills the key and told him that it was under the seat and that he'll get the car back from him later. J-Mills nodded his head got out and G-Rock pulled off.

J-Mills got in and started the car up. He reached under the seat and grabbed a plastic bag. Put it on his lap opened it and seen a brick wrapped nice and tight. It was his first time seeing a whole one before but it definitely wouldn't be his last. He called his dudes and they agreed to meet him at Reef's house. He was only around the corner so he was the first one there.

When they all arrived they went in and J-Mills placed the brick on the table and told them, "This is what we're working with."

Mir picked the brick up and felt how solid it was. J-Mills told Reef to bring him a razor, alumina foil and some zip lock bags. When Reef came back J-Mills put the coke on the alumina foil so if something fell off it'll catch it. The way he seen it they couldn't afford to lose a gram. He grabbed the razor and began cutting from the edges. The brick had three layers of wrappings. The first was like some brown tape, the second was some rubber waterproof stuff and the last was foil. It was two layers of coke, the top had a fish imprinted on it. They broke it up, weighed it up and put it in zip locks.

Afterwards they went and got Red. Red cooked the whole thing nine ounces at a time. They wanted to make sure they didn't mess up anything. They paid Red a quarter ounce and a hundred dollars and sent him on his way. Green was the color they chose to bag up in. They dropped everything raw and bagged up fat. The goal was to get things banging. They had three shifts, one worker each shift and took turns being out there with him. Sometimes they all would be out there. They was bringing everything back to the table before splitting the profits.

Coup and Plus didn't see them as a threat. Their main money was powder and weed. They not only had a powder flow that came to the block but they had big drops who be wanting quarters, halves, and ounces. They kept them away from the city so no one else could run into them. Only the crack was 24/7 and they hugged that thing like they were emotional wrecks. It took about a month and a half but the block went from doing a brick every week and a half to doing a brick every three days.

Eventually they put some weed out there too. G-Rock told J-Mills whatever he wanted so J-Mills took advantage of the opportunity to have another revenue stream. They went from having one worker out there to having multiple with multiple drugs.

They were young boys getting money so the first thing they brought was some new toys. Reef copped a Chrysler 300 SRT, Pooh a Grey Charger, J-Mills a Chevy Malibu, and Mir snatched up a Yukon Denali. They smacked tint around all of their cars except Mir. His came with factory tint except the two fronts and he didn't want to put tint on them because he wanted people to see him in it.

G-Rock really took a liking to J-Mills. He liked the way he moved. He was a natural born leader. Kind of reminded G-Rock of his manz Rich who had gotten killed a few years ago. The fact that he was Melo's nephew just made his resume even more solid. G-Rock kept his manz Melo abreast about his nephew. Melo trusted that he was in good hands. Him being a part of the mob was destined. Not only was he hearing about his nephew from his manz but also dudes in prison was talking. Mostly all was good except when they talked that the word was he killed Little Man. Even though Little Man was Melo's dude it wasn't anything he could do but hope that his nephew didn't get locked up for it.

J-Mills was in tight with G-Rock and Row. He had gained their trust and they were showing him things that not many was privy to. J-Mills began seeing things from a different perspective.

Things were as G-Rock said they were. Everything out there was going through him either directly or indirectly. Not only that, him and Row was treated like celebs wherever they went.

One night they attended Fat Chop party at Plush Night Club over Philly. It was packed with professional ballers, and rap stars. Row introduced J-Mills to his manz Fat Chop.

"I remember you, the camera man, right?" Fat Chop smirked as he shook J-Mills hand.

"This Mr. Entrepreneur right here, jack of all trades," Row said with his arm around Fat Chop's neck like they were best buddies. The champagne he was drinking had him tipsy. Fat Chop started talking and from the door J-Mills knew what kind of dude he was. He prided himself on being a good judge of character. He definitely knew a dick riding slimeball when he seen one and no doubt he felt that was Fat Chop. To J-Mills somethings just wasn't right with this guy, but Fat Chop wasn't his manz so he brushed it off.

"You got this shit jumping in here," Row told Fat Chop trying to yell over the music.

Yeah, if you don't leave with some pussy tonight you gay," G-Rock said to Row joking.

"Fuck out of here, you know ma dick stay wet," Row shot back.

"Let me introduce you to ma manz J-Mills," Fat Chop said and called Craze over. Craze was a Chicago rapper who was becoming big. He had a couple hits out that was getting a lot of play. G-Rock and Row already knew him. While everybody was talking like they were childhood friends J-Mills eyes scoured the club and landed on this shorty nearby who was wearing all white.

She had a nice ass and her pants were extra tight, they made her ass look that much more enticing. She had her back turned talking to her girlfriends. J-Mills was looking at her ass as if he had x-ray vision. He was trying to figure out if she had on a thong, G-string, or no panties on at all. He was in a trance, he didn't notice her looking over her shoulder at him. Her girlfriends had peeped him and had put her on point. He had his drink in hand, eyes low pissy drunk. She started wiggling her ass for him but he was in a zone and didn't realize that she was doing it for him. She turned around, he looked up and seen her coming his way. He tried to wipe the stupid off of his face as she walked up to him close enough to smell the champagne on his breath.

"You like what you see," she asked? J-Mills licked his lips like he was L.L. Cool J and smiled flashing his pearly whites. That always melted chicks, but he was really smiling at how she was coming at him. He couldn't help but to notice how beautiful she was. She was dark skin and short just how he liked his women. The way she walked over to him in them heels spoke wonders. He knew she was stepping into his life.

Without answering her question he took another sip of his drink and asked her, "what you got on under that?"

With a little smile she said, "It's only one way to find out."

"Enough said, what time you leaving?"

"Whenever you ready," she responded.

J-Mills admired her confidence, but she didn't know what she was getting herself into, or maybe he didn't know what he was getting himself into. He got Angie's name and number and they agreed that she'll be right there with her friends when he was ready. He told her to give him fifteen minutes. He turned around and started talking to the fellas while she went back to where her girlfriends were at.

"She got a stuffy (fat ass), and a mean walk," Row told J-Mills when he came back over there.

"Yo you pissy drunk right now, you might can't handle that. She going to be taking her clothes off and you going to be sleep like an old man," G-Rock said clowning. They all started laughing.

"I got something for that," Craze said pulling out an E-pill. One of these and you going to put on."

"I don't mess with them E's," J-Mills said.

"I only dump them when I'm trying to really get right. You hit her off of this she going to be forever yours, trust me."

J-Mills always stayed away from the pills because he heard that there was dope, crack and a bunch of other mixture of drugs he never wanted to use in them.

****

"Can you drive," J-Mills asked?

"Of course."

Aware that he was too drunk he handed Angie the keys. Plus that pill had him feeling like he never felt before. The whole ride he was feeling on her, he couldn't wait to get to the hotel. Bout time they got there he was sweating with a dry mouth. He could have made cotton with the white stuff he had on his tongue. As soon as they got in the room he went straight to the bathroom and started drinking some cold water out of the sink. When he came out Angie was getting undressed. She had a hot pink G-String on. To him it was looking like candy on her body. He was standing there like a dog with its tongue hanging out his mouth watching her undress.

"Come here, you look thirsty," Angie said as she sat on the edge of the bed. She sat there naked with her legs open. He stood between them and she unbuckled his belt and pants. He took his shirt off. When she got his pants down his dick was dumb hard, reaching out for her face.

"Dam," she said grabbing on it. "Get on ya knees," she commanded and like an obedient dog he obeyed.

She put her legs up and he started licking and sucking her pussy. If he wasn't on that E-pill he probably wouldn't even had ate the pussy after just meeting her but he was doing all kinds of stuff to her. Licking her ass and everything.

"O god, it feels so good." She was trying to get away from him but he kept pulling her back. Then her legs began shaking uncontrollably, she started humping his face while coming.

After he made her come he started hitting it, he really had her yelling for God then. They went at it until the sun started to rise. He performed like an Olympic gold medalist off that e-pill. Some of the things he did to her messed her head up. She thought he was possessed.

CHAPTER 10

The next day he woke up with Angie naked cuddled up with him. He was feeling hung over. He couldn't remember much from last night. His dudes were right, he passed out. The things they did was a blank in his mind, all he knew was that she was ass naked and his manhood was looking like Nasa had sat it up for takeoff.

He began thinking about Isha. Ever since they moved in together he always made it home. Even though it usually was late, then he began thinking about how he just had raw sex with this chick who he didn't even know. He moved and Angie woke up. She seen his man standing tall and grabbed it and started giving him head. After she finished blowing him with the stick breath he looked at his phone and seen all miss calls. On top of that it was almost noon. He jumped up got in the shower, came out and asked Angie where she wanted him to take her. To his surprise she said 30th street out east Camden. The whole time he thought she was a Philly chick.

Even though J-Mills and Isha never really argued when he got home he was expecting to hear her mouth. He was surprised to see she wasn't home. He changed his clothes and went around the way. Pooh was telling him how Isha had came through a couple times looking for him.

The block was low on coke. J-Mills had a half of brick left. Him and Pooh went to the cook up spot out North Camden on tenth and Cedar. A spot G-Rock had put him on. Not too many dudes knew about this spot unless they were getting money or of course unless they were from North Camden. That in itself made going out there a risk because dudes out there were grimy. It was only a half a brick so the intentions was to be in and out. They decided not to bring their guns this time.

J-Mills knocked on the door and this tall brown skin skinny fiend answered the door looking like Tyrone Biggums from the David Chappelle show. It was another fiend in there he knew name Gate. When they were coming in he was going out. Usually the policy was nobody in or out until they left, but J-Mills gave him a pass because he used to mess with his cousin back in the day.

Fee was a chemist, she could easily turn two into four. She came downstairs, she had her vision wear pots, ice and baking soda ready to go. J-Mills put two ounces on eighteen, plus a little something for Fee. He hit her with a hundred dollars and they were out. The car was across the street. Nobody was on the block except this old man who sat on the porch. As they walked to the car another car slowly turned the corner. It was a burgundy Altima. The fact that the windows were foggy for no reason had got their attention. It wasn't clear if they were thinking the same thing but if they were strapped they would have lit that car up. They wasn't strapped though. They both knew something wasn't right. That they had got caught slipping.

Everything seem to be going in slow motion as they kept their eyes on the car. J-Mills went to the driver side of their car and Pooh to the passenger side. The other car was going so slow that whoever was in it could have walked where they was going and got there faster, but it was no doubt that the car was coming for them. As soon as they reached the doors of their car the Altima cut in front of it so they couldn't pull out. The dude on the passenger side got out with an AK 47. He had a hood on and kept his head low so he couldn't be seen. Only from his nose down was visible. As he held the gun to J-Mills stomach J-Mills noticed a cut near his mouth. Dude didn't have to tell J-Mills to put his hands up, once he saw that gun he threw them up like he was being arrested. The driver jumped out without a mask pointing a dessert eagle.

"Ya'll know what it is," he said as he went around to the passenger side pointing his gun at Pooh who had his hands up too. They searched them and found the drugs. They also took money, and their keys so they had to walk back to Parkside. It was complete silence on that walk.

The first thing J-Mills did when he got to Parkside was go to the auto body shop so they could tow his car back. They did with no problem, they knew his money was good. It was one of his friends uncle's shop.

At the crib on Empire Street J-Mills kept playing the whole thing over and over in his mind from beginning to the end. Reef and Mir had gotten the call and came over. Reef was hot and wanted some action. He was also upset with J-Mills and Pooh because they should have known better than to go to the cook up spot without their burners. Especially without him. Reef was a cannon.

He got his first taste of blood when he shot dude from 32nd street years ago. Dudes was on this porch when Reef rode up on a bike with no shirt on. His shirt was hanging over the gun that was on his waist. They were having words about dude trying to trap on Chestnut and he wasn't from out there. That quickly escalated and dude began trying to back in the house, Reef pulled out his burner and started blaming dude then rode off on his bike like it was nothing.

J-Mills was also feeling some kind of way. It hurt being robbed. The loss plus being on the other end of the gun. Being a victim, watching his life flash before his eyes. They could have killed them but they didn't and that was all the motivation J-Mills needed.

He remembered the guy who didn't have a mask on vividly. He was sure he'd seen him somewhere he just couldn't pinpoint where. It was hard to see the other dude face.

After thinking long and hard in retrospect it finally dawn on J-Mills that the crackhead dude Gate who they let leave the house must have set them up. "He had too, he was the only one who knew we was in there," J-Mills said after telling his dudes what was on his mind.

They waited a couple of weeks before they decided to go back out there to see if they could catch somebody slipping. They rode in two cars, J-Mills and Reef in one car and Mir and Pooh in the other. They rode through 8th and 9th street, then through 6th and Bailey, that's where Gate sister used to stay. They didn't see him so they split up. Reef drove to second and front street and lo and behold there he was walking through the projects by himself, nobody else around. They got out and ran down startling him. Reef hit Gate with a Tyson style right hook that put him right down. Then he pulled out the burner and started brutally pistol whipping him. CRACK CRACK CRACK. Gate was screaming like a bitch. With every violent blow Reef hit him with took more and more out of that scream. J-Mills had to stop him. Not because he wanted to save Gate but because the way Reef was swinging that gun it might have gone off popping one of them. Before Reef stopped he grabbed Gate by the neck and hit him once again in the mouth with so much force it knocked four of his teeth out.

"Who the fuck was them dudes who robbed us? I know you set that shit up," J-Mills said. He was standing over Gate as he spat out blood and teeth. He sat on the ground, Reef had him sitting up by the neck. He slid the 45. Into his mouth. He didn't even have to open his mouth, the missing teeth made a good fit for the 45. to slide right in. Gate eyes got so big that they almost popped out of his head.

"Ok ok," Gate was trying to say with the barrel pressed against his tonsils. Reef took the gun out of his mouth so they could hear what he was trying to say.

"His name Mo Mo, he got a spot on 7th and York. Soon as Gate said that name it came to J-Mill where he knew he remembered dude from. He used to pull capers with one of his manz older brothers. They were dope head stick up boys who tried to hustle every now and then.

They tried to get the other name out of Gate but he swore that he didn't know who dude was. They believed him because if he did know he was going to take It to the grave with him. J-Mills tapped Reef on the shoulder giving him the green light to bust his head. Instead of shooting him Reef pulled out a screwdriver that he kept in his car instead of a knife so if he got pulled over the police wouldn't think anything of it. It was really for if something happened and he wasn't strapped he could use it as a banger and get busy.

Reef started banging Gate up in the stomach, chest, face, arms, wherever there was an opening. It was nothing he could do to stop him. Gate tried blocking some but when it wasn't going through it was hitting bone. Gate was moaning in agony. Reef was a big muscular dude, there was a lot of force coming behind every blow. *Who does that,* J-Mills thought to himself watching his manz go berserk. He didn't know his manz was bugged out like that. That day he found out that Reef really didn't have it all. J-Mills was glad that they were on the same team.

They jumped in the car, J-Mills called Pooh and told them to meet them on 7th and York. They met up and was back to back when they got around there. They seen Mo Mo walking down the street. He kept looking back that's how they seen that it was him. Grimy dudes are always suspicious of everything moving. It was no sneaking up on him. They pulled up hopped out and he took off running. J-Mills began banging at him, he fired back without looking. The women and children who were outside ran in the house. J-Mills and his squad was in between cars chasing and shooting at him. Conscious that they were in his territory they didn't chase him for too long. They hurried back to their cars and got out of there.

CHAPTER 11

That Friday Reef, J-Mills and one of their trappers Qua had went to Jumu'ah (Religious services for Muslims). Pooh didn't go that day and Mir wasn't Muslim. Even thugs pray is a true saying. Rather they do it in a religious form or not. Mob figures like Gotti used to attend Catholic Mass. They had to redeem themselves in some way in case there really was a hell.

After Jumu'ah J-Mills dropped his boys off then went to Bradley Street so he could meet G-Rock. He was the only one who re-up with G-Rock and Row. Even though the others was a part of his squad they was on some need to know basis. The less people knew what was going down the less risk it was for G-Rock and Row. They all respected that. When J-Mills went to meet Row on Bradley Street he had Fat Chop waiting in the car with him. It was understandable for G-Rock not to make it and Row come because they were partners but J-Mills wasn't cool with anybody being in his business.

When J-Mills walked up to the car Row unlocked the doors but J-Mills tapped on the window signaling for him to get out of the car.

"What's good little bro," Row asked as they shook hands?

"Chilling you know. No offence Row, I'm doing business with you, I can't make a move with O boy right there."

Eyebrows raised Row was a little shocked but he could do nothing but smile and respect it. He liked that J-Mills was on his shit. If anything he would of thought somebody like a connect would of said something like that not someone under him.

"Alright, I respect that. I'ma drop him off around the way and come right back. The whole time Fat Chop was in the car J-Mills didn't say anything to him. Row got in the car and took off. J-Mills got in his car took the dutch out of the ash tray, lit it and turned up the Young Jezzy he was listening to.

Row came back in ten minutes and they made the transaction.

"We all going out tonight so if you trying to step out hit me up," Row said.

"I might not be able to, I gotta handle some things."

Row understood completely. Business was always before pleasure. That was a moto broke dudes couldn't grasp. Row was in a position where he didn't have to do much. J-Mills was still up and coming.

****

It was still work on the block, the bricks J-Mills just got from Row was took to the stash house to be cooked and bagged up. Afterwards J-Mills decided to go see his mom. When he walked in the house she was sitting there smoking a cigarette with her legs closed looking lonely. Ever since he been getting money he always tried to make sure his mother was alright. Even though when he gave her money he knew he was helping to feed her habit. For him it was better than her selling her body to get high. Crack was one of them drugs that a fiend would do anything for. He tried a couple of times to talk her into rehab but the addiction had her.

"What's wrong mom," J-Mills asked as he sat next to her on the couch?

"Not much," she said then took another pull of the cigarette like she needed smoke in her lungs to breathe.

"I never seen you stay in one spot for more than a couple of seconds, now you sitting here watching T.V., something wrong."

Anybody who knew crackheads knew that they were always on the move. Not only was she sitting still but there was no one else in the house. She always had company.

"I haven't had a hit all day," she said looking J-Mills in his eyes.

"That's good, you ready for rehab?"

"I don't know, but I'm tired. I told everybody don't come over no more."

"I think you ready. I'ma call them people tomorrow morning." J-Mills had got a call from Angie and excused himself to talk to her. When he hung up his mother was just looking at him.

"It's amazing how much you've grown. It seem like yesterday you were just ten."

J-Mills laughed a little. He knew that was probably the last time she wasn't high that's why it seemed like that. He left his mom's house hoping she was really ready to change her life for the better.

****

When he got around the way the block was banging. He seen Pooh and Reef in front of the Chinese store. Pooh was getting his car washed by this fiend name Archy.

"These dudes going out tonight ya'll trying to go," J-Mills asked?

"Nah, I got something lined up for tonight," Pooh said.

"She got a friend for me," J-Mills asked?

"Reef the one plug me in. I'm trying to see how these things looking," Pooh said. "In fact, I'll be right back. Pooh went in the Chinese store to buy some condoms. "What the fuck is this," Pooh asked looking down at the condoms? "Come on China man, you aint got no trojans or magnums back there?" The condom they were selling looked like little balloons.

"No no magnum," China man said.

"Well give me ma money back, I can't put ma dick in these. I'm the black man. Ya'll better start getting some official condoms, ya'll aint going to sell none of these around here."

CHAPTER 12

J-Mills and Angie had gotten together a few times after the initial night they met over Philly but this was the first time he been to her house. She had her own spot, it was very nice he noticed as he went on a tour. He been to plenty of chicks houses that was filthy. That was how he found out if they were dirty or not. He was pass the stage of falling for what a chick had on when she went out. While touring her house he was really making sure they were the only ones there and wasn't nobody trying to rob him.

Angie cooked a meal, while eating they were getting to know one another. J-Mills mostly did all the questioning. He found out that she was the daughter of a decan. Her family was heavy into church. Growing up she sang in the choir. Her father was strict, he knew the environment they lived in wasn't the best so all she was allowed to do was go to school, church, and attend family functions. Which explains why him nor any of his dudes heard about her. If she was a hood rat no matter where she was from in the city at least one of his dudes would had known her.

To be so young Angie had a lot going on for herself. She had her own home, hair salon, and a bunch of goals. She would get excited just talking about them. That's when he realized that she was different. J-Mills came to the conclusion that she was one of them square chicks who liked thugs.

He felt strange because usually when he cheated on Isha with another chick he would just smash, not spend time with her. Angie sex was so good that he came back for more. After that first shot it seemed like she was making him spend more time with her before he got some, that had turn into a thing. He didn't mind because he actually enjoyed her company. Plus after having sex with her he didn't feel like he just wasted a nut like he felt with a lot of other females he had sex with.

What J-Mills didn't know was that she had already knew about him from seeing him around in the city. He had already been the topic of discussion of her and her friends. Even though he was checking her out that night it was her who chose.

J-Mills sat on the couch while Angie stood in front of him slow dancing seductively to the Alicia Keys songs playing in the background. She began coming out of her clothes and instantly he could feel blood flowing from one head to the other. What females didn't understand was that when this happened all logical thinking went out the window. When little man got big he took over.

Angie's body was perfect, like God made her for himself. During diner she also told J-Mills that she ran track in high school. The truth was in the pudding. J-Mills took off his shirt, pulled down his sweatpants and sat back on the couch. He was about to put the condom on when she gently took it out of his hand. He didn't even put up a fight. She bent over and started kissing him. He slid down a little while grabbing his dick, insinuating for her to go on. She got on the couch and mounted him in a squat position. She held the back of the couch while squatting on his manz. Them track star legs held firm in this position. She slowly bounced up and down on him. For J-Mills it was a beautiful site but he wanted to switch positions so he told her to get up and bend over. When she bent over he had got a surprise he wasn't prepared for. She had gotten his name tatted big as day on her left cheek. He stood there with his manz in his hands just looking at his name on her. It had hearts roses and all these other designs on it. He didn't know what to think, it was so soon. One thing for sure was that whoever did it had skills, but he knew that she wasn't his girl so in his mind it didn't sit well with him that other dudes might be nutting on his name. He thought back to how when he would be having sex and a female who had another dude name on her how he would nut on it just out of spite.

Angie was looking back smiling. "This wasn't here last time was it?"

"Nope, I just got it, you likey?" J-Mills didn't answer. "I wanted to show my loyalty."

Loyalty was J-Mills favorite word. By her pledging her loyalty to him she became that much sexier. He could feel his heartbeat beating through his manhood. It was throbbing trying to tell him to go back in there so he could get the job done.

"So basically you telling me you mine?"

"I'm all yours baby."

"Say no more." J-Mills began long dicking her from the back. She was making porno noises. "Who pussy is this?"

"It's yours," she responded in between moans.

He had her saying his name as he talked dirty to her. When he felt himself coming he pulled out and skeeted all over her butt. *Fuck that, if anybody going to be bussing off on ma name I'ma be the first,* he thought to himself. They jumped in the shower and continued sexing. Before he left she gave him a set of keys to her house and told him that she meant what she said.

CHAPTER 13

G-Rock and Row went out clubbing with a bunch of their dudes. They was about seven cars deep. G-Rock knew the owner of the club they went to, they could have easily got in but that wasn't the plan. They just wanted to do some parking lot pimping. The lot across the street was packed. Dudes was posted up on their motorcycles and fly cars pushing up on the ladies that were drawn their way. G-Rock and his squad did the same. It was a different vibe from inside the club. Mostly every car in the parking lot was a foreign, or a motorcycle. They stood out there for a couple of hours smoking, drinking and talking to the ladies. Then they went to the gas station, it had a similar type of vibe but a smaller crowd.

Row ended up getting into it with Jean. Jean was from downtown Camden. They had beef a couple of years ago but it had died down. G-Rock and everybody else was chilling when some commotion broke out not too far from them. G-Rock didn't think it had anything to do with his peoples since they all were chilling. Then they heard someone say that it was Row, that's when they all rushed over there to see Row on top of dude Jean scuffing. Jean's dudes wasn't doing anything and Row was clearly getting the best of him. When G-Rock and his dudes ran over there they backed down. G-Rock pulled Row off of dude and they got out of there. They were only out there for like twenty five minutes.

"Him and his dudes pussy, and I took his watch," Row said smiling looking down at the diamond flooded Rolex.

The beef already existed but it was like a silent war. There was plenty of times that both squads could have got at each other but didn't. After what just happened G-Rock knew that would no longer be the case.

****

Row was sitting on the step on wildwood near the store. Other dudes was out there but he was sitting by himself looking in his phone. He was so into his phone that he didn't see Brand walk up until he was in his peripheral vision, that's when he looked up at him.

"What's good Row?"

"What's good Brand?"

"Why you out here slipping like this," Brand asked?

"How you figure that, look around you. You think nobody out here strapped?" Brand took a look around but still he knew that if something was to happen their reaction wouldn't prevent something that had already happened.

"O boy got some money on ya head. He tried to send me that's why I'm here." Row looked at him stunned at first not knowing Brands next move. "I aint on it like that though, you know you always been alright with me. I just came to tell you. I figure if I put you on point you'll look me out."

Row was relieved that he wasn't on it how he was sent to be on it. "You got a gun on you?"

"Yeah, he gave it to me to put you down with."

"What kind is it, let me see?"

Brand pulled it out of the front of his pants and gave it to Row. Row looked at it. "A 45. huh, he tried to take ma head off with this." Row took the clip out and seen that it was loaded. He put the clip back in then checked the chamber and seen that it had a bullet in it. He figured if Brand had cocked it back then he had it in mind to get at him but didn't have the balls to complete his mission when he got there.

Brand stood there watching Row inspect the gun wondering what he was thinking about. It never occurred to him the dumb move he made by giving Row his gun fully loaded.

"Come on, let's take a walk," Row said getting up from the step with the gun pointed at Brand's face.

"Oh man Row, come on man, forget everything, you don't have to give me anything. Please, just let me leave."

Row had led him down the alley, all the while he had the gun to the back of his head. They stopped when they got to the back of Sues Chinese store. "Turn around," Row said. Brand turned around with tears in his eyes. Row didn't show no mercy. "You should of did what you set out to do. Either way you dead. If I don't kill you now he going to kill you later but I want you to send him a message.

"Anything you want," Brand said.

Boom Boom! Row shot him two times in the face and a couple more times when he hit the ground. By bodying his so called hit man he wanted Jean to know that he was next.

CHAPTER 14

"Pull over at the store so I can get some Dutchess," J-Mills told Pooh. They both went in the store on 10th and Ferry. J-Mills was sitting in the passenger side with the door open. He cracked the dutch and poured the tobacco on the ground. Pooh was standing on the outside of the passenger door. While they were talking J-Mills rolled up some Purple Haze.

"What's up," this little boy asked when he walked up? He couldn't have been more than eight or nine.

"What up little man," Pooh said.

"Can I have some money," the little boy asked with no shame? Pooh started digging in his pockets.

"I be wanting to sell drugs but dudes be talking about I'm too small, but they don't be grown either." Little Man was blatant.

It was nothing for a young boy they knew to ask for money but his mother never told him not to talk to strangers. As sad as it was to most young boys growing up in Camden drug dealers were their role models.

"What's ya name," J-Mills asked?

"Ron Doe," he said.

"Rondo," J-Mills asked?

"No Ron Doe, it's short for Ron Doe Ski."

"Oh alright, I got you. Why you wonna sell drugs, you don't have any dreams?"

"Nah, I just want to have a fly car, money and some bitches. The girls be fronting on me now but they going to want me when I start selling drugs. Especially when I cop a chain, they going to be on me."

Pooh gave Ron Doe fifty dollars. His eyes lit up like a kid playing a new video game but that didn't excite kids in Camden like the fast life did.

"What kind of sports do you like playing," Pooh asked him?"

"I'm good at basketball. I'm always at the courts," Ron Doe said talking about the courts on 9th street.

J-Mills added another fifty dollars to the fifty Pooh already gave him and told him to stick to playing basketball that it'll take him a lot further in life than drug dealing will. A car rode buy with two dudes in it looking kind of hard. J-Mills and Pooh was on them.

"Come on, let's get out of here before they get us confused," Pooh said.

Row and G-Rock had beef in the city and they were becoming known for getting money with them. That right there automatically made them apart of their beef.

While they were riding J-Mills was thinking about how he was when he was younger. He wanted to be a drug dealer too. That's kind of why he felt like he couldn't really offer Ron Doe any positive advice. Plus the fact that he was living negative. It just wouldn't feel right trying to school someone while he was still living foul.

"It's crazy how the hood is, right," J-Mills said looking at Pooh who had the dutch to his mouth pulling on it with one hand with the other hand at twelve o'clock on the steering wheel. Pooh began nodding his head while blowing out smoke.

"The messed up part is that his mom probably fucking and sucking everything moving. She don't know shit so she can't teach him anything. His dad probably dead or in jail so he going to be lost. He don't have any guidance. We aint role models, we told him not to do something he know we out here doing. It's not what comes out a person mouth that kids listen to it's what they see that person doing."

Pooh kept going in about why things were the way they were. He was more conscious and smarter than a lot of guys his age but smart and conscious people don't always do smart and conscious things.

CHAPTER 15

J-Mills opened the door for Mir. Mir walked in and sat the bag of money on the table.

"What's good with you," J-Mills asked?

"Been chilling bro."

"You been kind of distant lately." J-Mills seen that Mir had been drifting, chilling with dudes outside of their squad, partying. J-Mills was big on discipline and loyalty so he felt like he had to speak on the way Mir was moving because he knew Mir lacked discipline. J-Mills was the type who felt that you couldn't only think for yaself but that he had to think for others too.

"I been around. I just be messing with the chicks or playing the game, I'm good though. Yo, I know you heard the detectives had snatched Row up." J-Mills raised his eyebrows because he hadn't heard that. He had heard somebody had got bodied out there a couple days ago but that was it. "He out now though. He said they questioned him about the body that dropped around there the other day and mention that they knew Jean had a hit out on him."

"What he tell them? That's always my question."

"Nah, I think he solid. He didn't get charged with anything but you know how people are always speculating or just hating throwing stuff in the air."

If Row and G-Rock wasn't the plugs J-Mills would have fell back from them because he knew they were hot. They were flashy and violent. That was the kind of ingredients the feds liked. It was no secret that they had been dodging them boys for some time.

****

Pooh had smacked one of Coup workers and took his drugs for trying to sell crack. Coup must have gotten a call because him and Plus hopped out extra tough.

"Fuck is good," Coup said as he called himself stepping to Pooh. Pooh sat on the steps talking to a couple of is soldiers, Case and Main. There were other dudes out there but they were in front of Tasha's house. Pooh stood up as he seen Coup aggressively coming his way. Pooh and his soldiers were strapped, they weren't worried, they were ready to bang out.

"What's good is that ya'll sell powder so stick to that."

On hearing that Coup looked at Pooh like he was crazy. He didn't care about their squad or who they were getting money with. He wasn't about to let somebody who he was older than by about ten years tell him what he couldn't do on a block he help start and let them on.

"I sell what the fuck I want out here. Me and ma dudes started this thing. Ya'll not even from out here. Fuck is wrong with you." Coup and Plus seen that the block had started banging for crack, all of a sudden they had started putting crack out there.

Pooh listened nonchalantly. Coup and Plus were both bigger than him but he wasn't afraid at all. He knew that size wasn't going to determine the outcome. Main and Case was posted up waiting for one of them to act stupid. They knew Coup wasn't like that because he wasn't on point. Plus was on point but even though he had his gun on him he had fear all over his face. He knew he wasn't ready to pull no trigger.

Pooh was the more laid back dude out of his squad. He like to get money and mess with the ladies. He wasn't with the nonsense, yet he handled his business every time he had to, that was principle.

"Like I said, stick to the powder. Anything other than that ya'll know what it is."

Pooh gave the smoothest warning ever. If it wasn't directed at Coup he would have definitely admired it, but because it was directed at him he was furious. Coup's face had gotten red, his nose flared up. He wanted to do something but he wasn't stupid. It made him more furious that he was losing control yet Pooh was so calm. Him and Plus got back in their car and sped off.

Pooh knew they weren't going to stop. He pitied them because he knew if they didn't then the situation was going to escalate. All they had to do was get out of the way.

In many ways the drug game is like sports but worse. In sports like football, basketball, and boxing every year is like five years because of all the stress one puts on their body. With all the smoking, drinking, stressing, sex, partying and killing dudes definitely become old before their time. In a profession where guys enter as early as the ages of ten or eleven, thirty and older is considered to be an old head.

****

Later that night Coup and Plus had their trappers down the street on Louis and Liberty as if that was going to make a difference. Like Pooh predicted they didn't stop anything. The smokers were roaming around like zombies down there. The strip should had been called crackhead lane. It was Camden's skid row.

Coup and Plus Workers were cutting off the flow from going up the block. They was out there supposedly watching their workers back but Coup was at the window of some car talking to these chicks. Plus was on the steps counting the money his worker had just given him. They must have thought the young boys was sweet because they were slipping.

Reef pulled the Jason Hockey mask down and put his hood over his head. Pooh had the Michael Meyers Halloween mask. They bailed out of the alleyway going straight for their targets. Coup never seen it coming, the chick in the passenger seat did, she started screaming. Once the first shots rang out the driver sped off.

Ducking his head Coup tried running with the car, he fell and got back up. Pooh dumped a few more in his back but he kept running dodging in and out between cars. He was able to get away. Plus was stuck when Reef ran up on him. He put his hands out as if he was trying to stop what was about to happen. He seem to have been trying to say something to plead his case but Reef began hitting him up. Everything happened fast, all the people that was out there scattered leaving Plus on the step slumped.

CHAPTER 16

"Fuck is wrong with ya'll, how we going to get money with a dead body on the block and the D.T.'s running around here asking questions? Think man, ya'll supposed to know better than that." Pooh and Reef sat there like two little kids that knew they did something bad while J-Mills was telling them how they messed up.

The death of Plus made Lib hot. For a while things slowed up but didn't stop. No matter where a person was crack sold itself. It could be raining balls of fire it didn't matter, if the coke was good the fiends was coming. They just moved their workers from Green Street to the Chinese store or to fresh donuts. Before that body dropped Liberty was a low key block, now the police made it their business to ride through there.

****

It was around six in the evening, the sun was going down. A bunch of dudes was on the block. The police came swarming from both ends of the block. They snatched everybody up, the only one who got caught with something was Little Nas. He had three bundles on him. The police kept asking where was the guns at. They said someone called them talking about they were out there with guns on them. They didn't find any guns. Little Nas went down but he was a juvenile, that was his first charge so they knew that he'll be right back out.

About ten minutes after the cops left Coup and the dude Pooh smacked up bent the corner guns blazing. Coup was really gunning for Pooh. He hit him four times. One in the shoulder, twice in the back and one grazed his thigh while he was running. Taj was on the block with them, he got hit in the leg too. Pooh and Taj got out of the hospital the same day. That shooting really made the block hot.

Lib became too hot to get money on. J-Mills and his dudes went back on Louis and Chestnut. Everywhere else out Parkside G-Rock and Row had on smash.

****

J-Mills pulled up got out and showed Rek some love first since he was the closest. "What's good playa," J-Mills said giving Rek a handshake and embracing him? It's been a while since they had a chance to interact. They were both doing their thing, in the same circle but wasn't as cool as they used to be.

"What's good," Rek responded flatly?

J-Mills wasn't feeling the handshake, embrace or his vibe. Everything felt weird. Ever since he murdered his cousin their relationship haven't been the same. He knew Rek knew just like he knew a lot of other people knew, but he thought nothing of it. *He could get it too if that's how he feel,* J-Mills thought to himself.

It's been months since Pooh got shot. Everyone was at Lubby's, a local bar. It was packed inside and out. G-Rock decided to stop the music to tell everyone that he was getting married to Joan. This nice little Puerto Rican chick he had been dealing with for some years now. He let everyone get a round on him. They all held up their shots and congratulated him and wished him success.

"I always knew this tender dick dude was going to be the first to get locked down," Row said jokingly after the announcement was over and the music was playing again.

"Fuck out of here, don't make me expose you," G-Rock said thinking about the chicks he knew who had Row open.

"You can say what you want, aint none of them ever get a ring. They just get hard dick and bubble gum."

"I know you going to have a bachelor party," J-Mills said.

"Of course, that's part of the agreement. I'm trying to break ma old record that night." G-Rock was talking about the record of how many females he had sex with in one night. His current record was five, so he say.

"We should take that show on the road to Atlanta. Ma uncle own Magic City." Pooh had been meaning to shoot down Atlanta for some time to see his family. He figured if G-Rock had his bachelor party there he could kill two birds with one stone.

"That sound like something, we're there," G-Rock said.

****

Two weeks before the wedding they chartered a jet and flew out there. It kind of messed J-Mills up that they chartered a jet. J-Mills thought they were going to catch a regular flight. Turned out nobody had to pay anything. J-Mills knew their money was up but not that they were moving like that. Altogether it was about fifteen of them on that flight. J-Mills, Pooh, Reef, Mir, G-Rock, Row, the so called jack of all trades Fat Chop, Rob and Duby, who had Morse street and another spot in front of this pizza store called Torelli's Pizza. Money was there, him and his squad had division and a couple other spots downtown. Cain, Tre, and Will had the Circle out White Boy Fairview. These were a few dudes Row and G-Rock dealt with around the city. J-Mills and his dudes didn't know any of these dudes personally until the day of the flight.

When they first touchdown everybody went to their rooms and roamed the city separately. For most of the dudes on that flight going to Atlanta was regular, they knew spots and had chicks and family down there already. For J-Mills and his dudes the only one who been down there before was Pooh. All the rest of them was new to the scene. Pooh had spent off to go see his family.

That night they got VIP in Magic City. It was ass good lord once they stepped in the club. Magic City was Atlanta's hottest strip club no doubt. Nothing but pretty sexy thick chicks worked in there. Reef and Mir was trying to put their fingers in every pussy that danced on them. They were trying to treat it like it was one of them Philly spots. In the strip clubs up north dudes be fingering broads and they got little rooms you could slide in with the strippers if you wanted to pay for a quicky. None of that was allowed where they were at. That aggressiveness almost got them into it with the bouncers. Pooh's cousin who worked there had to come defuse the situation.

J-Mills was enjoying himself at the same time keeping an eye out for his dudes. They were drunk moving way too aggressive. They kept ordering bottles, the waitresses kept bringing them waving the lights with the sparkles flaring. A couple dudes they were with ordered five thousand in ones. It came in a black duffle bag, bricks of ones. They was acting up in there, making it rain having a good time. Magic City was used to this type of action. At the end of the night they snatched up some strippers and some chicks that was in there. That night G-Rock failed at breaking his old record, he was having too much fun to worry about it.

CHAPTER 17

G-Rock had his wedding at a mansion that he rented off of Air BNB. The estate was about a block long. A lot of people was in attendance. G-Rock family and all the top dudes he got money with. Joan's family was there deep. She had all these bad mommies in her family. J-Mills couldn't help but to push up on one. She was looking like a young J-Lo when her ass was still fat. He spent most of his time there with her trying to figure out what she was saying. Her English was chopped like she was fresh off the island. She was killing him with that sexy accent. It was like she was speaking a different language but he knew what she was saying. On top everything she was so cute.

While she would be talking he'll be looking at her like he wanted to eat her. She was just smiling and blushing. She told J-Mills that she was from Puerto Rico but lived in Miami. J-Mills knew that he might not get a chance to see her again so he was trying to smash but she was politely turning him down. He figured if they weren't at the wedding he probably could have smashed. They had switched info though. For her he was going to take that trip.

The wedding was beautiful. The whole thing seem like something out of a fairytale. G-Rock had to have spent an arm and a leg putting it all together. Fat Chop was the camera man. He did all the wedding photos and had his manz, some fat white dude he said worked for his company recording everything. After getting married G-Rock and Joan had their honeymoon in the South of France.

****

J-Mills wouldn't have dared taken his girl to a wedding. He could see her trying to be slick and catch the bouquet. He told her that he was going on a trip and she automatically assumed that it was street business and didn't ask any more questions.

Angie had become his number two. She was getting quality time but he had stop having sex with her raw because he didn't want to get her pregnant plus the thought that she might be dealing with someone else was always there. He wasn't eating the pussy or hitting it raw so he didn't think much of who else she dealt with because she wasn't his girl, even though she clearly wanted to be. He didn't like when she would ask questions about his girl. That was a subject he was always trying to avoid.

Since G-Rock was on his honeymoon the next time J-Mills had to re-up it was with Row. They were fly and everything was on the up and up, it's just what Mir had told J-Mills Never left his mind. J-Mills felt for Row to be a boss that he moved kind of sloppy. From the time he tried to make a move with Fat Chop in the car, to him killing dudes around where they be. None of that was boss like in J-Mills opinion.

The heat had died down from when Coup and Plus got shot. Liberty was back open doing numbers. J-Mills squad also had Louis and Chestnut. Both of them blocks were doing good for them but they knew they could be doing a lot better but all the surrounding blocks G-Rock and Row had. Their competition was their connects which wasn't beneficial to their ultimate growth.

CHAPTER 18

"Ok, what do we have Mr. Scott," asked the overweight white DEA agent?

Fat Chop started spreading the recently develop pictures across the table. He had videos of the wedding and other evidence of him and Row making transactions. There was a billboard on the wall of dudes from all over Camden who Fat Chop had been taking pictures of. The bosses were on top and under every boss who was under them. The accuracy was to a tee, all curtsey of Fat Chop.

For years Fat Chop had been given the feds information on dudes throughout the city. It first started when he got pulled over and the cops found four bricks of coke and a gun. The feds approached him and ever since then he had been their eyes and ears helping them put all the pieces together. A lot of indictments extended from his cooperation and nobody knew because he never had to testify. Dudes thought when he was taking them pictures that they were just flicking it up, little did they know.

The feds had been trying to build a case on G-Rock and Row for some time now. They recently had gotten enough to pin Row but they also wanted G-Rock and everyone else he dealt with. They were casting their net wide. The feds rarely took down one person even when they knew they had enough to put that person away. They like to take down organizations, that's exactly what they were trying to do.

"From my observation of things, he definitely starting to hold a lot of weight," Fat Chop said pointing to J-Mills photo. He had been snitching for so long now that he started talking like the police. Only around them though, because when he was around hood dudes he would act hood. A true imposter, which was why he had got in that position in the first place. "He young but I can tell the way he move that they respect him, even G-Rock and Row. I don't think he likes me much though."

"I hope that's not the reason why you picking him out," said the fat agent as he stood leaning against the desk eating his jelly powered donut. "So where should I put his photo at," he asked as he grabbed the picture with his powered fingers?

"Put it in the second row with the other guys that's under G-Rock and Row. Put these ones under his." Fat Chop handed the agent pictures of Reef, Mir, and Pooh.

"I assume the shootings on Liberty Street happened over a drug dispute. The only reports we have are from three crackheads saying they seen two guys with mask on," Agent Lynch said looking at the other officers waiting for a response.

"They would have told us anything to get that forty dollars we gave them," Agent John said.

"I believe either of these four had something to do with it because, it's their drug block, so they think." Agent Lynch was the one heading the investigation. He never went in the field until it was time to make an arrest. He evaluated all evidence from his office.

There was silence as Agent Lynch looked over all the photos trying to put things together. Even though everyone in there knew that what Agent Lynch was saying was probably right it was no way for them to prove it so they didn't speak on it.

"What about him," Agent Lynch asked referring to G-Rock? What do we have on him? He's the big fish we're really trying to catch."

"We got him on audio and video but not saying anything dirty or incriminating," his fat subordinate said.

"Alright, I need you to get me something on him," Agent Lynch told Fat Chop.

"I say we lock Row up now and once he sees all the evidence we have on him he going to tell us everything we need to know to take everybody down," Agent John suggested as he went to go sit down. He seemed anxious to put these guys in prison.

"It's not going to happened that easy. I know Row, he really live that life, he's not going to give his friends up. This is a grown man that knows the consequences of his actions. He's willing to die in them streets or spend life behind bars before he go out like that." Fat Chop knew Row well. He was warning them that if they raid now that they'll blow everything, at the same time he'll be exposed. He didn't want that. He was supposed to be a confidential informant, meaning he wanted to keep it confidential.

"I understand you think he's like that," Agent John said quoting with his two fingers for emphasis. "That he's going to hold up the G-code or whatever," he continued in his extra white sarcastic voice. "How many so called gangsters do we know who broke the code, including you?" Fat Chop was silent. "I rest my case. They all gangsters until they're facing thirty to life then they start thinking about the next man putting his thumb in their girl butt. This gangster you speak highly of, wasn't he just hiding from a hit somebody had on him?"

"Who wouldn't," asked Fat Chop?

What nobody knew was that it was Fat Chop who told the feds about the hit that Jean put on Row.

"We're going to wait until we get more on the rest of these guys so we could make a clean sweep, eventually somebody a start talking, they always do," Lieutenant Lynch said.

With that said the meeting was brought to an end.

CHAPTER 19

J-Mills couldn't have been happier for his mother. Today was the day she was going to rehab and he was in the process of dropping her off. The GPS led them to a house in Penns Grove New Jersey. It was a six month residential program that his mom was entering. J-Mills was willing to pay more to keep her longer if she needed it. He just wanted to make sure she was good. She knew whatever she needed he was only a phone call away.

When they got out of the car she was looking scared like a little girl on her first day of school.

"I wish you the best mom. You know if you need me for anything just call me."

"I know," she said as they walked towards the entrance.

A lady waited for them in the doorway. Before J-Mills mom went in she turned and gave him a hug. Initially he was kind of shocked, he couldn't remember the last time his mother hugged him. He hugged her back and they held each other for about a good minute.

"I love you."

"I love you too mom."

J-Mills started to become emotional. The thought of his mother getting herself together was becoming more and more a reality by the second.

"Hello," J-Mills said answering his phone. He was on his way back to Camden when he received a call from Cortney. She Messed with this dude from McGuire projects but she always cheated on him. She wasn't one of them smuts that let dudes run trains on her but the dicks had piled up on her over the years. Recently her dude had gotten locked up and she needed to get pounded that's why she was calling J-Mills.

"Where you at?"

"I'm on ma way to the hood. Why you trying to bless the god," J-Mills asked joking?

"You gotta come over now because I have to go get my kids soon."

"Alright, I'm there."

When J-Mills got there Cortney aint have anything on but a towel. Her long legged and brown skin was an instant turn on for him.

"What ya freak ass doing in here with no clothes on," J-Mills joked?

"I just got out of the shower boy." She went into attack mode and started kissing him. She took the towel off and let it drop. She went down on him and sucked him so good that he came in about five minutes. They went in the bedroom and made the house shake for about forty minutes.

"You about to start paying for the dick, you aint going to keep using me every time ya dude get locked up," J-Mills said joking.

"You know you ma bitch," Cortney responded.

"I'ma remember that next time."

J-Mills chilled there until she had to go get her kids. After leaving he rode through Louis and chestnut. He stopped and talked to a couple of dudes. Everything was running smooth. The next stop he made was through Lib. Lib was doing numbers. Seeing Mir and the fellas out there he pulled over.

"What's so funny," J-Mills asked seeing them laughing?

"I was just telling Mir about the time Reef took me over these big chicks house. These chicks were extra wide, but his was cute. Mine looked like Resputia from that movie Norbit." Reef was laughing extra hard while Pooh was telling the story.

"He hit though," Reef said.

"Hell yeah, I don't turn down nothing but ma collar."

"I was ripping her big ass. She was making all these ugly ass faces, all that just made me go harder. I'ma still get you back though."

"Ya boy blew through here. He was in his Bentley today," Pooh said talking about G-Rock.

"Yeah, I gotta get me one of them. They really doing it on another level. They flew us out there in a jet," Mir said shaking his head smiling.

"Yeah I know," J-Mills said rubbing his chin looking like he was brain storming.

Reef was leaning against the car with his arms folded and Pooh was sitting on the hood.

"They really doing it, they make the few bricks we moving look like crumbs," Pooh said.

"We supposed to be doing it like that. We gotta turn it the fuck up," Mir said. Mir was the flashy loud type. He loved stuntin and being the center of attention. He wasn't the type that ran his mouth about their business though. He was just flamboyant.

"You right, that is supposed to be us. Everything out here supposed to be us." When J-Mills said that they all looked at him like they were anticipating his next words.

Reef gave a devilish grin as though he knew what his manz was thinking, which he did, they all did. "I'm saying we can make that happen, it aint hard to do. We already in position. The hood already look at you like you the next Don. We rock them and everything is everything," Reef said.

J-Mills knew what Reef was saying was right but what's the use of taking over the whole hood if you couldn't supply it.

"They got a mean connect. They getting them things for real cheap," J-Mills said while trying to come up with something. "We going to make it happen though. They old asses in the way of what could be big business."

J-Mills had made his mind up. He wanted Parkside and it was only two people in his way. The thing was they had to do things without bringing heat on themselves and avoid beef because he knew they were feeding a lot of dudes and when you mess with dudes bread and butter they gone want to eat you.

CHAPTER 20

"O ma god girl you glowing," Kim said all loud and excited.

"You looking good too girl," Isha said responding to Kim's compliment.

They hugged as though they haven't seen one another in years but it only been about four months. Kim was Isha's friend and hair stylist. They grew up together. They were in the salon loud and excited, all eyes were on them.

"You know who that is," Tammy asked Angie?

"No, who she supposed to be," Angie asked with a face and tone of voice like she could care less. She kept doing her clients hair.

"She mess with J-Mills, that's his girl," Tammy said.

Angie tried to conceal her emotions but her face said it all. Still she played it off while really checking Isha out on the low. Finding out that she was J-Mills girl peeked her interest. Now she was looking for flaws, trying to see if Isha had anything that she didn't have. They were similar in many ways, they just didn't look the same in the face. Angie had seen her come in the salon before but never paid her any mind.

Angie's salon was kind of big and Kim's area was close to the door. Angie and Tammy's areas were in the middle but they was trying their hardest to ear hustle in on Kim's conversation with Isha.

"You must be going somewhere special because I haven't seen you in some months. Kim was wondering why Isha haven't been coming through how she used to.

"I had gotten some braids. I had them in for a minute, I kept switching styles that's why I wasn't getting my hair done."

"Who did them," Kim asked?

"The Africans in Philly."

"So where you going and with who, I want to know everything?"

Kim was washing Isha's hair out while Isha filled her in on the last few months of her life. She told her that J-Mills was taking her on a cruise to the Caribbean. She talked about how the cruise was supposed to stop at three Islands in five days.

"Girl, why you getting ya hair done? You going to be all in the water, plus you going to sweat it out having sex."

They both laughed. Isha knew she was right, like she told her she just wanted it done for some of the pictures they were going to be taking. For the next couple of hours while getting her hair done they talked about everything from family, relationships, to episodes of Hip Hop Atlanta.

The whole time Angie was listening furiously heart broken. Tammy knew it too, she didn't even say anything to Angie. Angie knew J-Mills had a girl, he kept it a hundred with her but for it to be thrown in her face like this gave her an indescribable feeling. After hearing about the trip he was about to go on Angie went in the bathroom and texted J-Mills. "Don't call me when he come back from your cruise with your girlfriend. I tried but I can't do this anymore."

****

"This bitch buggin bro."

"What happened," Reef asked?

"Nah, this chick Angie going to text me talking about don't call her when I get back. She knew I had a girl, I don't know why she on some bullshit. I don't got no time for this shit," J-Mills said before taking another pull of the dutch. He didn't bother to text her back but then he got to thinking. "I should go fuck this broad to calm her down. This is why when you cheating you have to just stick and move. They be getting all emotional and if you get emotionally involved it's going to mess ya situation up."

"Man them chicks know what it is with dudes like us. I don't even know why she tripping. That's why I mess with the one I got. She might not be the prettiest but she got her shit together and she don't give a fuck what I do as long as I come home she don't ask no questions. Plus she got that stuffy," Reef said and they both started laughing.

"Ma chick don't ask questions either, it's just this broad."

Reef turned on to Walnut Street and their little man Rap had flagged them over. He was looking distressed.

"Yo, Wan just robbed me. Him and this big dude."

"Yeah, get in," Reef told Rap. Which way did they go?"

"They went the doghouse way."

"What they driving?"

"A Black Cherokee."

"They headed to one of them dope spots," J-Mills said.

They rode by a few nearby dope spots but it was no sign of them so they headed back to Parkside.

93

Dudes was deep all up and down The Ave (Haddon Ave). J-Mills got out of the car and started talking to G-Rock. Rap went and told his manz what had happened. He was waiting for Nut to show up so he could tell him what happened. Nut ran Walnut Street for G-Rock.

"This dude Wan Robbed one of Nut young boys," J-Mills told G-Rock.

"Who," G-Rock asked?

"Rap, right there."

"Nut going to handle that. Wan probably don't show his face for a couple of months, you know how his bitch ass is."

"What made you bring this thing out," J-Mills asked referring to the Bentley?

"I aint buy it so it could just hold a parking spot."

G-Rock had a grey tinted up Bentley GT with black rims on it. They sat there talking for a little. J-Mills was trying to make another move before he went on his trip so they was to get together that night.

CHAPTER 21

That weekend Isha and J-Mills left for their vacation. The cruise liner itself was a moving Island. It had everything on there, from clubs, restaurants, tennis courts to pools etc…. Kim was right because bout time they made it to the first island which was Dominica Republic Isha's hair was a done deal.

They went sightseeing, scooper diving, jet skiing and did everything romantic they could think of.

"We have to do this more often babe."

"You right, this living. Soon it's going to be like this every day for us. I'ma make sure of it."

"You real romantic when you not in the hood or fronting for ya boys."

"Stop playing with me before I bite you for real this time."

They had just finished eating and was sitting across from one another holding hands.

"What's next," J-Mills asked?

"I wonna see the dolphins," Isha said.

"Alright, let's go."

J-Mills act like he was getting up but then sat back down.

"Boy get up and come on," Isha said pulling his arm.

"Give me like thirty seconds," he said rubbing his stomach.

****

Isha was in the water with the dolphins petting and kissing them. J-Mills participated but Isha was into it way more than him. Either one of them had ever played with a dolphin before but she acted like she never played with a dolphin before. That's how excited she was.

After they left from the dolphins they took a walk on the beach. J-Mills was very conscious while playing in all that water because he couldn't swim. He kept telling Isha if his feet couldn't touch the ground then he wasn't going out there but Isha kept trying to pull him deeper into the ocean.

"Come on," she said pulling on him.

"Stop playing."

"I knew you was a punk."

They were already about three feet in but she was trying to get him to go further. He kept fighting her, then he slipped and his head went in the underwater. He jumped up real fast like he was about to drown. He took a deep breath wiping his eyes. Isha was laughing at him. He grabbed her, picked her up and took her to about six feet of water and dunked her under then ran out of the water. She came out of the water still laughing at him.

"Allll you mad," she said. "Come give mommy a hug."

That same night they went to the casino that was on board and gambled some money. All while there they did a bunch of activities and enjoyed each other's company.

CHAPTER 22

When they got back to Camden it felt different, like they was on another planet. It seemed like it was always a dark cloud over Camden. The air smelt different and the dudes were always mean mugging. On their trip everybody looked beautiful with smiley faces. They didn't hear any sirens from police cars, ambulances, or fire trucks. They had been in heaven for them few days, now they were back in hell.

J-Mills was back in the hood up to his old ways. The islands were paradise but it was nothing like the hood. This day he happen to be coming out of this chick house on Princess Ave when he seen G-Rock parked, sitting in his range rover by himself talking on the phone laughing it up like he didn't have a care in the world. Technically G-Rock and J-Mills were manz but the griminess of the game turned best friends into strangers. J-Mills had plans and getting G-Rock out of the way was a part of them.

He contemplated on what to do. This was a rare opportunity. He couldn't believe G-Rock was slipping like this. It was around twelve midnight and it was a ghost town out. J-Mills didn't even see any trappers. He decided that he was going in. He wanted so badly to call his dudes but he couldn't wait. They might not have gotten another sweet opportunity like this one again.

He jumped in his wheels and turned up wildwood then down Kenwood Street. Still nobody so he figured the timing had to be perfect. He pulled over and grabbed the black hoodie out of his back seat, put it on and got out leaving his car running. He hit the alleyway creeping at a fast paste. He knew the alleyway like the back of his hand being as though he grew up playing in them when he was younger.

J-Mills peeked around the corner of the alleyway onto the street and saw G-Rock was still there on the phone and the coast was clear. He pulled the 45. From his hip, checked the chamber and started jogging real low close to the cars until he got up to the Range Rover then he popped up looking like The Reaper. G-Rock dropped the phone and put his arms up trying to cover his face as if that was going to block the bullets. J-Mills started letting him have it, about ten shots in total. While running off he heard movements in the distance coming from somewhere else. The whole time it was two dudes on the porch. He didn't see them when he first rode through. He sent a couple shot in that direction without looking back. He ran to where his car was waiting and got out of there.

****

"I think they killed G-Rock," Rek said trying to catch his breath after they stop running. He had both hands on his knees looking at Wez who was trying to catch his breath also. He was leaning against someone's backyard gate scared to death.

"We gotta go back," Rek told Wez as he pulled his gun out. They started heading back but wasn't going nowhere near as fast as they was when they heard them shots.

Rek had become one of G-Rock's most trusted manz. He ran Princess and Wildwood for him. When they got to the Range Rover G-Rock was still in there fighting for his life.

"O shit, I got you. I'ma get you to the hospital." Wez helped Rek get G-Rock to the passenger seat. Rek gave him his gun and told him that he was going to Coopers.

****

While in the waiting room at Cooper Hospital Rek was making phones calls. First to G-Rock's Wife and mother then to Row. Out of all three he called it was hardest to break the news to Row. He knew how his attitude was.

****

Row was 6 foot 3 260 pounds all muscle. He was a linebacker in his high school days and was offered multiple scholarships for football and could have made it to the pros but opted for the instant gratification and thrill of the street life, not to mention the money. He figured that he was already living the life he wanted to live.

Row was in some good pussy when he got the call. His girl Tyra was off to the side a little riding him, biting her bottom lip looking back at the movement of her own ass. His hands were rubbing her ass and tits.

His phone went off, he went to grab it and Tyra tried to stop him. "I need to get this baby girl," Row told her. Tyra started pouting because he was blowing her groove. He didn't care, his philosophy was (MOB) money over bitches. A philosophy that he believed if more dudes lived by they'll get a lot more money. She just kept riding him.

"Hello."

"Yo, they tried to kill G-Rock," Rek said hysterically.

"What, who?" Row blew Tyra stuff for real when he got up from under her in the middle of her doing her thing.

"I don't know who."

" Where he at, Coopers?"

"Yeah, that's where I'm at too."

"I'm on ma way," Row said before hanging up the phone. "I gotta go, you wonna stay here or you want me to take you home?"

"I'm staying here," Tyra said.

She had plans on finishing the job he started. She didn't even wait for him to leave before she started playing with herself.

Row put on his clothes and left. When he got to the hospital the emergency room was packed. It looked like the inside of a refugee camp. He spotted Joan (G-Rock's wife), Rek, and G-Rock's mother at the far end of the waiting room.

"How they say he doing," Row asked?

Joan and G-Rock's mother was sitting there looking sad and concerned. He didn't even bother to speak to them. They had one worry in mind and that was if G-Rock was going to survive.

"We don't know yet, he still in surgery," Rek told him.

Rek and Row had stepped to the side. The only thing Row wanted to know was who was it so he could get revenge.

"You still don't know who it was," Row asked looking down on Rek as they stood up facing each other? Rek was about four inches shorter than him but he could clearly see the anger in Row's red watery eyes.

"Word up, I don't know big bro. Me and Wez was on the porch waiting for traps to come through and dudes just started shooting. They was bussin at us too, we got out of there," Rek said nervously as he tried to explain how everything went down.

"Was ya'll strapped?"

"Yeah but….."

"But nothing mothafucka, fuck you got a gun for if you not going to use it," Row said cutting Rek off.

Rek couldn't say anything, he just put his head down because he didn't want to make Row madder than he already was. He looked like a child who knew that they had did wrong.

In his head Row was going through the process of elimination of who could have wanted his manz dead. They had put in so much work over the years that he couldn't think of just one source. All he knew was that he better be on point because if they wanted G-Rock then they wanted him too.

"Excuse me Ms. Brown." G-Rock's mother and Wife stood up to meet the black doctor with the clip board in his hand. "I would like to inform you that Garen Brown has survived."

"Thank god," G-Rock's mother praised the lord then hugged Joan.

The doctor continued. "He's in critical condition right now and there is a chance he might be paralyzed. One of the bullets hit his spinal cord."

CHAPTER 23

"As salammu alaykum (Peace be upon you)," Reef greeted J-Mills with the Islamic greeting after J-Mills got in his car.

"Wa alaykum salam," J-Mills said returning the blessings.

"Yo, somebody hit G-Rock up last night." Reef thought he was delivering some good news after that discussion their squad had.

"It's all in a days work," J-Mills proudly said while putting the weed in the dutch.

"Dam, that was ya work? Why you aint come get me?"

"I caught him slipping and couldn't resist."

"I heard he paralyzed now," Reef said.

On hearing that J-Mills was disappointed in his gun work. He thought he finished him off. He Knew things could get ugly if anybody found out that he was the one who did it. G-Rock had all the power in the hood and everyone would take his side if there was ever a beef between them.

"The block banging too," Reef said interrupting J-Mills thoughts. "I guess because it's hot down there all the smokers are coming up here. The detectives all down there asking questions. We going to need to re-up soon too. I think these dudes ready for you too," Reef said referring to Mir and Pooh.

J-Mill and Reef had went to their stash house to cook up some more work. After that robbery incident they didn't go back to the spot out North. They had learnt to cook up for themselves.

****

A few weeks after G-Rock had got hit up Rek was out east at the liquor store when he ran into Bush from Phifer. He was inquiring about G-Rock being as though that was his manz.

"He alright, getting better every day. Right now he trying to lay low and recover."

"Tell him if he need any extra shooters let me know. I aint forget how he looked me out. I still feel like I owe him."

Some how they got on the subject about Little Man which was Bush's manz also. Rek still being bitter and holding animosity in his heart towards J-Mills started filling Bush in on the details. He was hoping somebody got at him or snitched, it didn't matter to him. The kind of details he was giving up definitely could get J-Mills life in prison. Bush knew about J-Mills but didn't know him. Once he heard that he was the one that killed his manz he put him in the category with the rest of his enemies. J-Mills had no idea.

CHAPTER 24

"Mir, what's good playa, what you doing in here?"

"Getting a little upgrade to ma system." Mir said responding to Fat Chop who was at the register talking to the clerk.

"What you got something new out there, because I know you already had a bang in ya wheels?" Fat Chop went to the door and looked outside. "That thing right there nice," Fat Chop said after seeing Mir's apple red 760 BMW.

"What made you get that color?"

"I don't know. I aint want to keep getting the same colors that everybody else be getting. White, black, silver, tan, I had to switch it up."

Fat Chop nodded his head in approval. "I feel that."

Mir told the store clerk what system he wanted in his car. The clerk told him to bring his car around to the garage so they could get to work. While they worked on his car Mir and Fat Chop stood outside smoking.

"How G-Rock doing," Fat Chop asked?

"He good, we still trying to find out who did that shit. If you get wind of anything let one of us know, somebody gotta feel it," Mir said as he pulled on the dutch and blew out purple haze smoke knowing dam well his manz was the one who did it.

"I'm saying everything still everything right," Fat Chop asked trying to see how much would come out of Mir?" He already knew that everything was still the same, he just was trying to get fly with Mir.

104

"He aint dead, he still moving out."

"I asked because I haven't seen him in a minute." Before Mir could respond Fat Chop had gotten a phone and excused himself for a second. "That was ma little freak," he said after hanging up. "She got this bad cousin. I'm going to put you in with her, alright?"

"Go ahead, I don't turn down no pussy."

"Alright, I'ma give you a call when I set everything up. Ma little chick bad but when I seen her cousin I was like dam. She blowing ma little chick out the water."

"I trust ya judgement. Just give her ma number and tell her to hit me," Mir said.

When Mir's car was done they said their peace and went their separate ways.

Mir wanted to make sure his new car was right before he came through the hood in it. When J-Mills seen it he was pissed off but didn't say anything. Mir parked in front of Fresh Donut entrance on the Haddon Ave side. He wanted everybody to see it. Mir's flamboyant style often had dudes see him as a joke which led to him putting hands on a few dudes who thought he was sweet. He didn't mind catching rec, he invited it but going out and having a good time was really his thing.

****

A couple days later Mir had gotten a call from the chick Fat Chop had put him in with. Her name was Ashley. He was on his way to meet her at the pub near the circle. When he got there he didn't know who to look for. Out of nowhere he heard this sweat low voice call his name. He walked over to her and tried to hide how stunned he was. Her beauty was undeniable. He could tell she was older, about thirty five he figured but still not too many young girls he knew had anything on her.

"Mir, right," Ashley asked?

"Yeah, how did you know it was me?"

"Chop described you to the tee and so far I'm not disappointed," she said smiling.

A big smile appeared on Mir's face but she was lying the whole time. Ashley was really Special Agent Katrina McNeal. She was brought in for one reason only and that was to get close with Mir so she could find out what she could about their squad. She knew exactly what Mir looked like from seeing the pictures of him that her superiors had her study.

"Did you order yet," Mir asked?

"Not yet, I was waiting for you."

They called a waiter over and placed their orders. The whole time while talking she fed him lies from a script that was given to her. It had Mir fooled though. His initial thoughts was that Fat Chop was plugging him in with a piece of pussy but as their conversation flowed he wasn't seeing her as just that. It was something about their conversation that made him not want to try her on the first day. Usually he'll take a chick to the drive through and head straight to the motel or hotel. All signs were indicating that this wasn't going to be one of them nights.

After they ate he paid for the meal and walked her to her car. While walking her to her car he was a step or two behind her checking her ass out and how it sat on her back like Sarina William's. Before she got in her car they hugged and Mir couldn't help but to palm them cheeks. She smiled, then he asked for a kiss. She gave him a peck on the lips.

CHAPTER 25

The Sun had set and the streetlights had came on. J-Mills was riding through East with two of his young boys Main and Case. They turned down Pfeiffer Street and begin hearing gun shots. First thing that came to J-Mills mind was that they just got caught in the middle of crossfire. He didn't have beef with anybody on Pfeiffer that he knew about.

He sped up trying to get out of the mix. They could hear the bullets hitting the van but they couldn't really see where the bullets was coming from because of the tint. Then J-Mills felt something hit his back. He knew he was shot but he didn't panic. He was focused on getting out of there. The adrenaline was blocking him from feeling any pain.

"Fuck that, let's get out and bang out," Main said trying to open the sliding door. Main was young and impulsive, that combo always kept him in something. J-Mills probably would have been inclined to do that but he couldn't being as though he was shot.

"I got shot," J-Mills said.

"Where," asked Case who was sitting in the passenger seat?

"In ma back."

Main was sitting in the back seat, he began lifting J-Mill's shirt up so he could see where he had gotten hit. "Dam, you leaking bro. You gotta get to the hospital," Main said after seeing how much blood was coming out.

J-Mills turned left on Baird Boulevard and crashed into the back of a car. A lady and two kids were in it. She was trying to get out of the line of fire also. The crash wasn't anything serious he bounced right off of that car and zoomed over the East Camden Bridge.

When they got to the hospital J-Mills told Case to take the guns and leave. Case didn't want to take any chances in the bullet riddled van so he took his shirt off, wrapped the guns up and started walking.

J-Mills was getting dizzy before they went in the hospital, once they got in there and the bright lights hit him he started thinking about the other side. Main was yelling telling the hospital staff that his manz had gotten shot. A nurse brought out a wheelchair for J-Mills and took him to the emergency room. All of a sudden J-Mills was feeling the pain more than ever. Probably because the focus was now on the womb.

It seemed like moments after they got there Isha and her mom had arrived. Ten minutes later the detectives showed up trying to catch J-Mills when he was most vulnerable. They like to catch dudes while they were doped up, in pain, or about to die so they could make an unconscious or an emotional decision and snitch. A lot of guys fell victim to this strategic move but not J-Mills. While getting operated on he was taking all the pain he was feeling out on them.

"Do I look like a snitch?" The detective didn't say anything. "Get the fuck out of here and go do ya job. Why would I make ya job easy for you?" He was talking filthy to them and this made them mad.

"I hope you die," one of the detectives said on his way out.

When they got outside they seen the van which was right in front of the hospital exit. They didn't pay it any mind on their way in but they knew a van had been involved. From all the bullet holes they figured it must have been the one. While searching it one detective found a gun under the seat. He held it up showing his partner.

"Looky looky here what I done found."

After they finished searching the van they went back inside and handcuffed J-Mills to the railing of the bed.

"What the fuck you doing?"

"You under arrest ass hole. We took your advice and went and did our job," the detective who found the gun said.

"What did he do," Isha asked? She was demanding to know what was going on. The detective was more than happy to let her know that he found a Glock in J-Mills van.

Glock, no this guy didn't leave his gun J-Mills thought to himself. He was disappointed that Main had forgotten one of his guns. He couldn't do anything but prepare to hit the county once he was released from the hospital.

CHAPTER 26

"I really appreciate you saving ma life little bro," G-Rock sincerely told Rek. G-Rock knew if Rek hadn't come back for him that he would be a dead man.

"It's nothing, I feel bad that I didn't see it coming I would of gave it to him."

G-Rock put a little smirk on knowing Rek wasn't built like that but that wasn't why he had him under the wing. He knew and understood that everyone has a position to play. He had him because he was focused, trustworthy, and loyal. They were all rare qualities in the game.

"Would ya'll like anything to drink," Joan asked while on her way to the kitchen?

"Yeah, bring something for the both of us baby."

It's been months since the shooting and G-Rock haven't left the house much. Beside his family he only let a few people who he got money with come see him and J-Mills was one of them. He didn't trust many people. He still didn't have an ideal who was behind the shooting. He figured it was his enemies but he didn't know which one. Then it was always a possibility that it could have been somebody who he was getting money with who didn't want to pay up. All he knew was that whoever was trying to get at him wanted to finish him off and would more than likely try again if they had the chance.

"You see that bag right there," G-Rock said pointing to the Footlocker bag that was on the side of the couch where Rek was sitting?

Rek picked it up and looked in it. It was two bricks of coke and fifty thousand dollars in there.

"What you want me to do with this," Rek questioned?

"That's you."

"Dam, good looking bro," Rek said still looking in the bag.

"You save my life. You the reason I'm able to wake up and see ma kids every day. To me that's priceless, that's the least I can do to show ma appreciation. I'm really thinking about leaving the game but I haven't decided yet. No matter what I'ma make sure you good. Until then we going to keep the same routine. See Row for everything, he know to look out for you."

It was nothing for G-Rock to give Rek what he gave him and a piece of Princess and Wildwood. Rek was still getting coke from them so the money was coming right back. Rek sat there taking it all in. He was already getting money and had more than the average hustler. That's because the average hustler just be trying to get by. What he was just blessed with was easily over a hundred plus stacks. That on top of the position he was given was a major boost. It was a heavy load, he wasn't sure if he was ready for the responsibility. In his mind he questioned himself while they talked but of course he couldn't let G-Rock know that he was thinking on some bitch shit. He knew G-Rock would have messed around and taken everything back.

****

Mir and Fat Chop was doing more hanging out than ever, going to clubs, messing with different chicks together. Fat Chop was one of them Fat Fly dudes who like to throw money around so when he came through the ladies seen dollar signs more than anything.

Fat Chop made it his business to try to avoid J-Mills. Mir knew J-Mills wasn't feeling him so he never brought Fat Chop around. Mir was the only one in their squad who went out with outsiders. Pooh, Reef, or J-Mills would never go anywhere unless they were moving out together. They knew how Mir was though.

Mir had been seeing Ashley for some months now and they have been having sex. She always made him wear a condom telling him that she wasn't ready for kids yet. For her to let him hit showed how far she was willing to go to accomplish her mission.

Ashley presented herself as the wifey type. He had fallen head over hills for her. Mir tried doing his homework on her but couldn't find anybody who knew her. That was a good thing because that meant aint nobody have any dirt on her. She carried herself like a lady and treated herself like one. She told Mir that she was originally from Paterson New Jersey but moved to Gloucester to take a job as a guidance counselor at their high school.

All Fat Chop told Mir was that she was his girl Saundra's cousin. That he met her a couple years ago and that she was good peoples. Mir didn't think much of it, he took his word even though he never even met Fat Chop's girl Saundra.

CHAPTER 27

B.O. came home fat. It was obvious he didn't bother doing any working out while he was in locked up. He made his rounds and seen that his block was not the same. Half of the dudes out there now he didn't know. Things had changed in the two and the half years he'd been gone.

B.O. had got with Rek and Rek filled him in on everything that had happened since he left. Who got Louis and Chestnut now and who killed who. Most of that stuff B.O. wasn't worried about, he was just trying to get money.

"So that's all J-Mills out there now?"

"Yeah, they messing with G-Rock now too. We alright but I don't really deal with them how we used to. They be on their own shit."

"What they be on some Bullshit," B.O. asked Rek?

"Not really, it's just after J-Mills did that to Little Man I fell back from him. The rest of them rock with him so you know. I'm saying I still speak, aint no beef or anything."

"I feel you. I'm trying to get to that bag, I aint worried about nothing else."

****

The next day B.O. went to Liberty for J-Mills. When he came through the young boys ran up on him like he was a trap.

"What's up unc, how many you want," one young boy asked with his whole stash in his hands?

"Dam, I look that bad," B.O. asked touching his own face? Before that moment he thought he was shining with a prison glow. "I aint no fucking fiend, where J-Mills at?"

"He in that car down there," the young boy said walking away from him.

"Which one?"

"The black one."

When J-Mills seen B.O. walking up he started smiling and tucked his money. He got out of the car to greet B.O..

"Oh shit, What's good bro?"

"I'm good, you know trying to get right."

"Yeah, that's not a problem nowadays. Whatever you need let me know."

J-Mills had no problem putting B.O. back on, even giving him a spot on Louis and Chestnut. B.O. would just have to get the coke from him. They were discussing them details when Reef walked up. B.O. and Reef embraced each other really happy to see each other.

B.O. was amazed to see how much they had come up. Their whole squad started under him. While B.O. and Reef was talking J-Mills went in his car, counted out fifteen hundred from the money he was counting and gave it to B.O. so he could get whatever he needed.

"Good looking bro."

Reef pulled out a couple of dollars and hit him off too. About fifteen minutes later B.O. left. J-Mills and Reef was posted on the side of Donkey's talking when a car full of ladies pulled up.

"Ya'll got weed," one of them asked?

"Yeah, pull over we got all the dick you need," Reef joked.

J-Mills started cracking up. Reef told the young boy who had the weed what they wanted.

"Get out of the car," Reef yelled. Once he seen who was in the car he knew who he was going to hit that night.

"Nina," Reef said making her look his way.

"Oh hey Reef, I didn't even know that was you." Then she started looking at J-Mills to see who he was.

"Hey J-Mills," she finally said after seeing that it was him.

"What's up Nina," J-Mills said back.

Nina was a freak from back in the day. She had them by a few years. When she was going around giving that thing up they wasn't really in the mix like that so they kind of missed the chance but Reef was on her. Her ass was extra bouncy while she was walking over to the young boy to get the weed.

"What ya'll about to get into," Reef asked?"

"Nothing, we going to Tianna house to smoke," Nina answered blushing. She was on him on as much as he was on her. She had been hearing things about him and his squad that peaked her interest. Now to know that he wanted her only made her like him even more. "Why, what you doing?"

"Nothing. I'm trying to see you tonight."

"Alright just call me," Nina said.

Reef pulled out his phone to lock her number in his contacts.

On boring days J-Mills a usually go home early and chill with Isha but lately he been spending more time with Angie. That's where he ended up going to cool out at. He used his key to get in. He walked in and seen Angie on the computer, he gave her a little kiss on the forehead then went in the kitchen to get something to drink. When he came out of the kitchen she had dropped everything for his attention.

"Can I get a massage," he asked on his way upstairs?

Angie was with whatever he wanted. That was always a super plus in a man's mind.

"You real tensed baby."

"You'll be real tensed too if you lived the kind of life I live."

J-Mills laid on the bed while she sat on his butt giving him a back massage. When J-Mill first came home from the hospital his arm was in a sling. Where he had got shot he wasn't able to move his arm, but he heeled up fast like Wolverine. Within a couple of days he was back in commission.

He found out who did the shooting through word of mouth. The streets gave him up. Bush must have known because he went into hiding which was probably best for him because he was on everybody from Parkside hit list, except Rek's. He probably was helping him hide out.

Bush being in hiding didn't stop his manz from being victims. Reef and a couple other dudes blew through there like tornadoes trying to destroy everything moving. They shot a couple of dudes but nobody died. The detectives got wind that the shooting had something to do with J-Mills getting shot so they paid him a visit. They threatened to revoke his bail if they found out he had anything to do with the shootings. Besides that they really couldn't do anything to him. They left with what they came with which was nothing."

CHAPTER 28

Angie leaned in and started licking and sucking on J-Mills ear lobe. She knew that always got him rocked up.

"Turn around," she whispered.

She got off of him so he could do so. He already had his shirt off, she helped him take his pants off as if he was the chick. She grabbed his manz and started with the head, kissing on it and sucking it like a blow pop. From there she went straight to deep throating, bringing tears to her eyes. Every time she went down she'll squint and try not to gag. Every time she came up she'll open her watery eyes and look up at him to see if he was being pleased. J-Mills was loving her tenacity. He put his hand on top of her head so she could speed up the motion. After a few more minutes of head fakes she abruptly stopped and laid on her back.

"Come on, fuck the shit out of me."

As many times as she swallowed he couldn't complain that she stopped. He stood over her rocked up. He took the condom out of the wrapping and was putting it on. Angie sucked her teeth. She hated that he wore condoms with her like he didn't trust her. It made her feel dirty like she was going to give him something, not to mention also unworthy of his kids.

Angie wanted him and his kids and she was willing to do whatever it took to have them. Lately she had been bringing up Isha trying to get him to leave her. J-Mills had let her know that it was no way. That Isha was there with him when he didn't have anything, that she was his baby girl. Even though he cheated on her, she was his heart.

Everyday J-Mills had beautiful ladies with nice bodies coming at him. He wasn't trying to have them all but he wasn't trying to resist them all either. Angie knew the game she just wanted that number one spot. She wanted to be the one he came home to at night. She knew no hood dudes were faithful. If that's what she was looking for then she would have gotten a square, but she wanted him and was willing to accept whatever came with having him.

Angie was on her back pulling him down. His man needed no guidance. It inserted itself in the pussy. J-Mills had her legs near her head thrashing her. She assisted him by holding her own legs in place. Only a few minutes in of going hard the condom broke. J-Mills felt it break but he kept going. As he kept stroking the condom rolled back to the base of his manz. Her insides was already feeling good but raw it was feeling great. Two totally different feeling. For a split second he thought of pulling out but he didn't stop his motion. Now he had a reason to go raw. He was already in forth gear but once the condom broke he started poppin the clutch until he got in six. Within minutes he skeeted all in her.

Angie felt the warmness enter her body. As he was pulling out she was looking down while making a face like it was taking her joy away. She seen that the condom had broken. After J-Mills recharged they went another round, this time there was no condoms involved.

CHAPTER 29

It was a Saturday night Mir was in Luby's talking to this young lady who he was trying to leave with when Row came in. Mir seen him but acted like he didn't. He pulled out his phone and called J-Mills.

"Yo bro," J-Mills answered.

"Bro, O boy just came in here alone."

Without thinking J-Mills knew who he was talking about. They had already been talking about finishing them dudes and how since G-Rock wasn't as mobile that Row was their biggest threat.

"Where you at?"

"Luby's."

"Alright, don't let him leave."

"Say no more. How long?"

"About fifteen minutes. We just came over Philly but I'm turning around now.

J-Mills and Reef crossed back over the Ben Franklin bridge from Philly into Camden. They switched cars and went to go get Pooh and moved out.

Meanwhile Mir was with Row throwing shots back. Row was one of them dudes who didn't just like to drink, when he drank he liked to get pissy drunk. Plus he was a big boy so he consumed a lot before he really started feeling it. They both sat there buying shots for themselves and the ladies. Row drink was Henny, the ladies wanted mainly Remy, Mir was a Ciroc boy. Mir looked at his phone and seen the text he been waiting for. He gave Row a handshake and left him at the bar with the ladies.

****

J-Mills was parked near crown fried, about a block away from the bar. A perfect spot for them to see everything that came and went out of there. Mir got in the back seat and they patiently waited. Styles P Super Gangsta played real low. They wasn't listening to it though. They were strapped up and focused. All of them had silencers on their guns except Mir. If things went according to plan he wouldn't need to bust his gun though.

Row finally came out of the bar stumbling to his car. They was expecting him to have at least one of the ladies with him but him by himself was even better. As soon as he pulled off they did too. They followed him to Camerhill on 34th street where his main chicks Pam lived.

Row was taking his time getting out of the car which gave them enough time to run up on him. They came from both sides of the vehicle and started hitting it up. Row looked like he was getting something out of the armrest when the first shot hit him. He didn't feel any pain, just a sting. His shoulders flinched like he was doing the Harlem Shake. He looked up and seen two masked men, he tried jumping in the back seat to get away from the hot bullets that was penetrating his body. There was no escape. They left him slumped, half of his body in the back seat the other half caught between the seats.

They headed to Pam house. 34th was a quiet street and it was 1:00 in the morning so nothing was moving out there. They squatted on both sides of the door while Reef knocked. Still with his mask on Reef held his finger over the peep hole. Pam must have been expecting Row because she had a welcoming smile on her face when she opened the door. Of course that was until she seen a mask man with a gun standing where Row should have been standing.

She tried to slam the door but Reef pushed it real hard with his shoulder busting her in the nose with it. She fell to the floor and tried to scream something but Reef put the bear claws around her neck cutting off all noises. He mushed her face in the carpet pressing her already broken nose against the floor. She cried in agony. Reef held her there while the others ran through the house searching for money.

They seen a baby in one room sleeping. In another room they found fifteen thousand but they knew it was more somewhere. Pooh came back and kicked Pam in the ribs.

"Where the fuck the money at bitch," he asked after the kick?

Reef still held her by the neck. J-Mills knelt down to Pam and said real calm but in a tone that meant business. "Tell us where everything is or we going to throw that baby in the oven and make you watch it cook."

Pam must have known he was serious because she didn't play no games, she took them straight to where everything was. All she asked was that they spare her and her baby's life.

Row had a false bottom in the basement floor where he kept everything.

"Jackpot," Pooh said as he pulled up big stacks of money. All this paper, this gotta be at least a half of mil.

Reef held Pam up by the neck. She was crying, her face dripping blood and tears. It looked like if he wasn't holding her up that she wouldn't be able to stand. She looked like a puppet.

After they left Pam kept crying and trying to call Row but she didn't get an answer. She was worried that something had happened to him since he was supposed to had been on his way but didn't show up. Calling the cops didn't cross her mind because she knew that Row wouldn't want that. Instead she called G-Rock and told him what happened.

Early the next morning the cops had knocked on Pam's door. A lady who was going to work noticed the car with a bunch of bullet holes in it, upon a closer look she seen Row in the back seat dead. When Pam heard the news she dropped to her knees in tears.

CHAPTER 30

Rek pulled up to Princess and Wildwood. It was packed out there with people grieving the death of Row. Wez was telling Rek what he heard happened.

"They did em dirty cuz, hit him up like thirty times I heard."

The top dogs getting hit up had Rek scared. He didn't know what was going on. He knew they did a lot and had their hands in a lot but he didn't know anybody in their right mind who would go at them. For those same reasons the whole hood was stun.

G-Rock and Row had an untouchable mystic around them because they had a lot of love and a lot of respect where they were from. They also got money with a lot of killers which let other squads know that if they wanted sauce that they would have it coming from all directions. That alone stopped any nonsense. That mystic was gone now. The worse part was that nobody knew what was going on.

Later that afternoon Rek went to go see G-Rock. G-Rock had a nice house in Haddon field, not Far from Camden at all but in the cut. Joan let Rek in and escorted him to the backyard where G-Rock was at watching his kids play in the pool.

"What's good big bro, how you been?" Rek pulled up a chair next to G-Rock's wheelchair.

"You know, I'm living," G-rock responded.

"I know you heard about Row."

"Yeah, I had got a call from Pam like two in the morning right after it happened. She said they ran through there on some Gorilla shit."

"Did she say anything about who they were?"

"Nah, all she said was that it was four of them with mask." They both sat there for a couple seconds in silence. "It's Karma bro."

Rek looked at G-Rock as if he was speaking a different language. "Who that," he asked?

G-Rock smiled the whole time thinking, *these 90's babies don't know shit.* Then he began to explain to him that what goes around comes around.

"We did a lot of dirt and bodied a lot of dudes to get to where we got. Things like that don't get forgotten. Everybody don't get it handed to them how you did. We went hard, lost a lot and gained a lot. Me and Row was the last of all the dudes we came up getting money with. If they aint dead then they in prison and truthfully that's how it always end. The only way to beat that is to get out, aint no winners in this game. Shine while it's your time but you can't really trust nobody cause that dude you confide in a be the same one blowing ya head off for that paper or testifying on you when them fed boys come down with them indictments."

"Know that when you in this shit ya whole family in it because that's what's at stake. I know you might be thinking I'm just talking like this because I'm in this wheelchair but I had a lot of time to think and reflect and things been really hitting me. You see how them wolves ran in Row girl's house with their newborn baby in there. Now I look at ma kids and ask myself how could I keep putting them in danger like that. We don't be seeing the whole picture, we be too busy in the zone." G-Rock kept going leaving Rek drunk with all the drinks he was giving him.

Eventually every gangsta will have to hang his gun up and G-Rock was feeling like his day was near. He was tired of looking over his shoulders and trying to avoid prison. Him being in that wheelchair had him spending most of his time with his family. He really was learning how to value them more than ever. He knew if he ever got locked up that he was going to go away for a long time. With that in the back of his mind he still held on to the hood as though he owned it. In an instant his whole mood changed.

"This the life we chose though. I'ma have to make another pitching change since Row aint with us no more. Now you'll be dealing with J-Mills."

G-Rock had already figured out who was going to take Row spot. Rek looked at G-Rock, he wasn't feeling the move but concealed his feelings. He didn't want the position, it was too much pressure and he didn't like pressure. He liked to stay on the low and out of the way. He didn't have a choice but to go along with it.

****

Row's viewing was held at Carl Miller's funeral home in Centerville. It was so packed out there one would have thought a celebrity had passed away. J-Mills and his squad was there paying their last respects. For them it was nothing personal, they were just young and ambitious and knew that they could be getting a lot more money if they got the top guys out the way.

Row had on an all black suit laying there like he was at peace, even though one would assume with all the dirt he did that his soul would be going to the hellfire. J-Mills stood at the casket playing it off with a sad face as if he lost a friend. On the inside he was smiling until he thought he seen Row's eyes open and with the angry face his mouth say, "You snake mothafucka." J-Mills heart dropped and his temperature went up. He knew this couldn't be humanly possible. He squinted his eyes real hard a couple of times then took another look. Row was still laying there peacefully with his hands folded across his chest.

"Dam, I gotta leave that haze alone," J-Mills said to himself and walked away from the casket.

****

The next day J-Mills had came from Jumu'ah (Friday prayer for the Muslims) and went straight to the Echelon Mall. Echelon Mall had closed most of its stores but since nobody from Camden really went there like that anymore it was a good spot for J-Mills and G-Rock to meet up. G-Rock had told him that he had somebody important whom he wanted to introduce him to. Still playing the loyalist role he made sure that he was there on time.

In the food court J-Mills spotted G-Rock sitting with big Muslim, his name was Anwar. J-Mills had seen him in Jumu'ah not even an hour ago. He was wondering what he was doing there. He played it cool, shook their hands and salaamed the Muslim brother then took a seat. If this was the person of importance who G-Rock was talking about introducing J-Mills to then J-Mills knew he was more than just one of the good brothers who he always seen at the Masjid.

"I see ya'll don't need any introductions," G-Rock said rubbing his hands together. Then he made a hand gesture towards Anwar and said, "This is the big guy, this is who you going to be dealing with since Row is no longer with us.

They started discussing details, telling J-Mills about how many bricks, prices, and pick up locations. J-Mills was kind of surprised to find out that Anwar was the connect. All these years he knew the brother he never would have guessed. He ran security at the masjid. Anwar was an old head with a beautiful family. He had two wives and a lot of kids, all of them doing positive things and on their Deen. The brother was definitely on the low.

Since G-Rock couldn't do much and Row was dead G-Rock had put J-Mills in charge of meeting the connect and handling other important matters. J-Mills remained humble while loving how everything was falling into place for him. G-Rock had no idea how he was playing right into J-Mills plan. After making agreements on the arrangements Anwar left. That's when G-Rock began filling J-Mills in on the history of Anwar.

Anwar had been rich for a long time. He had a violent history in the city. Which was one of the reasons the feds use to be on him so much. He knew how to move so they never could touch him and as he got older and bigger in the game he fell more and more behind the scenes and the feds stop harassing him. Either they thought he gave the lifestyle up or they were waiting for him to slip up because the feds always like to keep tabs on dudes.

J-Mills figured that Anwar must of have had a Cartel connect because the prices he was giving G-Rock the coke for was the prices they be as soon as they get over the border. He caught an adrenaline rush just knowing that he was about to make millions.

J-Mills took Row spot and everything was going smooth. Every two to three weeks he was getting a shipment of eighty bricks of coke along with other drugs like weed, wet, and pills but his main focus was coke. Everything was basically his now. He delegated the weight sells to Mir, Pooh, and Reef. Instead of getting bricks for thirty he was now getting them for twenty six but he had to still give G-Rock his cut. For that reason he gave his squad the bricks for twenty seven and left them some room so when selling weight they could still beat the regular prices by a couple of thousand and still make money. It was a win win for everybody. Everything out Parkside they put on the ground and all that was coming back to them.

J-Mills worked his way in good with Anwar. Since they both were Muslims for the sake of Allah they had genuine love for one another. Anwar took a liking to J-Mills. He began schooling him on a lot of things like investments, businesses, property and having a family as a foundation. He told J-Mills that no matter what a man had if he didn't have a family he didn't have anything. That stuck with J-Mills.

J-Mills was getting more money than he could spend. He was taking trips with his squad to all type of foreign islands tricking off on the natives chicks while having a good time. He would also take Isha on trips so they could have their quality time and memories.

Mir, Reef, and Pooh did mostly everything. All J-Mills did was make sure they were on point, that the money was right, made sure the shipments was right and safe and that Anwar got his money. It never sat right with him that he had to bring G-Rock half of the profits. It hurted giving that money to someone whom he considered in the way.

J-Mills had been patiently waiting for the opportunity to put G-Rock to sleep for good. He thought about ghosting him (not paying) for the money and telling him fuck him to get it how you live. He knew G-Rock wouldn't be able to do anything himself, but even though J-Mills basically had control of the hood G-Rock still had a lot of love and loyalty out there. Plus G-Rock was still feeding a lot of dudes who wasn't from out their way just through him now. On top of that J-Mills didn't want Anwar to see him as disloyal.

That's a bad quality that can mess up a good relationship. An open cross on G-Rock wouldn't sit well with the people, plus that wasn't J-Mills style.

CHAPTER 31

Most of J-Mills free time was split between Isha and Angie. He was smashing other chicks too but he was spending so much time with Angie that she started to act like she had that number one spot. He always had to check her when she got emotional which was becoming her regular. He had stop hitting her raw because he didn't want to get her pregnant. They had an argument about that. J-Mills had thought she was over it but what he didn't know was when they were finished having sex she was taking the condoms in the bathroom like she was throwing them away instead she would empty them in her pussy. Even when he nutted in her mouth she would find a way to get it in her pussy. She was obsessed and determined to get pregnant by him.

He had become so accustomed to Angie that he would by her gifts for Valentine's Day and Christmas but he would only spend time with Isha on them days, taking her out to nice spots and doing lovely things with her. Angie wasn't feeling that, yet she dealt with it and still remained loyal instead of dealing with other dudes.

One of the only worries J-Mills had was his mom. She had came home from rehab and relapse. He had to send her back to rehab. He knew he had to get her out of the hood. Camden was the drug store for all South Jersey to go when they wanted some good drugs. It's where all the suburban white people came to get their stuff and where all the outskirt hustlers came to find good product for good prices.

Ever since Anwar had put J-Mills up on buying houses and fixing them up that's what he'd been doing. He didn't know anything about it, he didn't care what was wrong with them or how much they costed. He brought them, hired people and let them go to work. One spot he brought out Parkside he planned on turning it into a lounge. It was almost done. That was a spot he had big plans for.

Their whole squad had foreigns, everything tinted out. Mir took the cake when he came through in a baby blue Ferrari like the one Will Smith had in Bad Boys 2. Nobody in the city had a Ferrari. He always had to outdo everybody. J-Mills couldn't even feel any type of way because they were getting so much money that he started buying all types of stuff too. It's not like he was trying to shine it just became regular to be in nice things.

Mir let Ashley stay over one night, they made love and from then on it was like she lived there because she never left. He didn't mind he was in love. So much so that he eventually gave her a key. After that his whole house was tapped.

****

J-Mills days of playing the hood heavy was behind him. He had to do things from a distance, come through every now and then. Him and his dudes always got together to have a good time, besides the business they had going on together. They were still tight.

This particular day they had everybody come out to go to the basketball game in Centerville. The courts were packed with people from all over. J-Mills and his dudes pulled up and stopped the show. The back to back foreigns made everybody who was watching the game go straight to commercial. They were deep, iced out and strapped up. There was a couple of unmarked cars and a patty wagon out there. The police were always at these events seeing who was who while waiting for anything to jumped off.

They were out there for about an hour and a half socializing with the ladies and dudes they knew. A few people asked about G-

Rock, a few dudes wanted to know the prices. J-Mills was so far gone that he didn't like talking that talk anymore. Any new inquiries he let his dudes handle. If someone asked him he'll just look at them like they were speaking a different language and walk away. He was learning a lot about how to run his program from Anwar. He was already thorough but he was young and Anwar seen a lot of potential in him so he took it upon himself to school him along the way.

A couple of chicks J-Mills was talking to was trying to leave with him and get hit but he had came with his dudes and that's who he was leaving with. Beside Isha, Angie and a couple stragglers he caught every now and then he had fell back from hitting chicks in the city because they knew him and it was too much at stake now. With the position he held came a lot of changes. He was slowly embracing them but he was still young and there was still a side of him that was reckless.

Downtown had won the basketball game. They were all on the court excited. As soon as the game was over Parkside dudes began to leave. J-Mills was on his way out when he seen this dude posted up on the gate mean mugging. J-Mills was on him but really didn't pay him any mind. There was always haters some just wasn't good at masking it. J-Mills never seen him before. He walked by him and looked dude right in the face. He wanted to let him know that he seen him with the ugly face now he wanted to see if he was really like that. Dude looked away like he wasn't beat for a staring match.

"Mothafuckas bleed just like us," dude said.

J-Mills was still right there. All his dudes were around but he must have been the only one who heard him say it. J-Mills quickly looked around to see who else could he had been talking to. He aint see anybody but his dudes so he smack the shit out of dude almost knocking his head off. It was like the replay of a boxing match when somebody just caught a mean hook. Spit and blood came out of dude mouth. Everybody heard it, the whole crowd paused for a second. Once Parkside dudes seen what happened they began going on dude. The police started trying to apprehend people and break it up. Luckily nobody got locked up. After everyone from Parkside left dude manz ended up jumping somebody who aint have anything to do with nothing.

CHAPTER 32

That same night they went to a club over Philly. J-Mills had came back early, he had a few moves to make. On his way over the bridge he had gotten a call from Isha crying talking about somebody had tried to run her over when she had gotten out of the car. The car was speeding and swerved trying to hit her as she got out of the car. She dove back in her car so she wouldn't get hit.

When J-Mills got home she was on the couch traumatized, shaking with her head down folded on her knees with a gun in her hand.

"You alright baby," J-Mills asked as he sat on the couch next to her rubbing her back?

Isha looked at him with teary red eyes. He could tell that she had been shook up bad. She put her arms around his neck and hugged him tightly. She began telling him how for a couple of days she thought someone had been following her.

J-Mills felt bad thinking it was his fault that she was going through this. He knew he had to move and assured her they would. Getting the kind of money he was getting he was slipping having her mom still staying in the hood. No matter who you was or how much work a dude put in if he was really getting to that paper dudes was going to try something sneaky.

CHAPTER 33

Mir's mom was messing with this old head dude name Paul. He was a few years older than Mir's mom, probably in his late forties or early fifties. He drove a Cadillac CTS and blasted slow music every time he came around. They had been friends for some time but he wasn't an everyday figure in their house but he was allowed to come over so that meant something because Mir's mom was picky. For a while when he was younger he thought she was never going to deal with anybody after her divorce from his father. That would have been fine with him too but he did want to see her happy.

Him and Paul was cool. He kind of watched Mir come up but never tried to be a father figure, he just was this cool old head that his mom dated. They sat on the couch watching the basketball game talking about how many years left Lebron had in him and why as Mir's mom cooked diner.

Paul had watched Mir's evolution. His conversation and the way he carried himself was different, more mature. Even when he was younger driving his mom crazy and she would talk to Paul about it he never spoke on anything Mir was doing. Paul been knew what he was into but he could see that there has definitely been an upgrade in status. On the flip side Mir seen him as a regular ole Joe, just how Paul liked it.

"I see you like the finer things in life youngin," Paul said after watching Mir's diamonds put on a light show.

The change in conversation was unexpected but Mir was cool with that he was always willing to talk that talk. "Yeah, you know I just like to look good and feel good," Mir responded nonchalantly flexing his jewelry.

"I can dig it, you kind of remind me of myself when I was a scrap."

Mir wanted to tell him that he wasn't no scrap and that aint no way he could possibly remind him of him when he was younger. He didn't think that Paul could possibly be doing what he was doing when he was younger. So he thought.

"You think Lebron got another one in him," Mir asked trying to switch the subject back to sports?

Paul was done talking sports though, he wanted to talk caine. "How much you paying for your bricks?"

Mir started to feel uncomfortable. He wasn't expecting this conversation.

"I'll give them to you for 26,500," Paul said without even waiting for Mir's response.

Mir didn't know what to think. He didn't think he was the feds. If anything they would be trying to buy not sell he figured. On top of that he was talking 26,500. Them was better numbers than he was getting them for now. A quick thought of placing an order for the mother load then robbing him came to mind but then he would have to kill him and his mom would be sad, that wasn't something he wanted so he nixed that thought.

Mir began thinking of all the benefits of getting them for a little cheaper price. "26,500 huh?" That price was one that Was hard for Mir to pass up on. He knew he had to at least try him out. A straight line was hard to come by so when doors like that open one wasn't supposed to let them close. Even though he had a connect giving it to them for the low already you never knew when that well was going to dry up.

Mir decided that he was going to keep that connect to himself. It took him a week but Mir started dealing with Paul on the low. He was mixing stuff from him in with the other work he was moving. Just enough to keep Paul as an extra connect but not enough that any of his dudes a notice. He mainly tried to feed it to all the new people he was adding to his flow.

Their squad was built on loyalty. It messed with Mir's conscious a little to know that he was going outside of their circle but since Paul was so close to home he really felt like it was no way they could find out what he was doing.

CHAPTER 34

Angie pulled on Liberty looking for J-Mills. Nas went and got him. He was a couple houses down.

"Some chick out here looking for you bro."

"Who Isha," J-Mills asked Nas?

"Nah, some other chick."

Nas didn't know Angie. J-Mills got up to go see who it was.

J-Mills barely came through the block anymore so he couldn't figure out how she knew he was out there. Then he thought about it, his car. It was hard to miss.

"What you doing out here?"

Angie was out of pocket. She knew not to come through the block and she knew that he had a girl. He let her in so he wouldn't be seen with her.

"Why haven't you been answering my calls or coming over," she asked?

"I was just over ya house the other day."

"That was like three days ago and ever since you haven't been answering my calls."

Angie had become obsessed. Always wanting to be under him, calling all hours of the day when she knew he had a girl.

"I be having to fall back from you sometimes so when we get together it'll be special," J-Mills said holding her in his arms. He was hoping that she'll buy it but she didn't.

"Every time we get together it's special," Angie told him and leaned in with a kiss.

J-Mills had her ass palmed. She told him before that she always got wet when he did that so he knew she was wet. He looked down on her, his mouth near her nose. Luckily he wasn't one of them stink breathe dudes. She actually enjoyed the air that he breathed into her face.

"Who is that" she asked? "It sound like she being raped."

Angie was talking about the noise coming from upstairs. A couple of young boys was upstairs running a train on this chick, she was a screamer.

"I'll be right back." J-Mills went upstairs and shut the door. When he came back downstairs Angie was looking at him funny.

"That's what ya'll do at this house?"

"I barely ever come here. It might be what they do, I don't know. This spot for the dudes who be out here."

"How many of them up there with that girl."

"Just two."

"Just two, that's one too many. Anyway, you staying with me tonight?"

"I'll come over but I aint staying."

Angie sucked her teeth and folded her arms upset that she wasn't getting her way. She looked at him for a second then started walking to the door.

"You going to appreciate me one day," she said on her way out.

Between Isha and Angie J-Mills was rarely dealing with other females how he used to. Trying to please them two became a full time job. Angie was aggressive and never satisfied. She had started wanting to go places and do things how regular couples do. J-Mills really liked her so he would take her out of town. He treated her good but not on Isha's level and that's what she had a problem with.

CHAPTER 35

The next night J-Mills got up with G-Rock to give him his portion of money. It infuriated J-Mills when he had to take him this money but he played it off like it was love. Blinded by false loyalty G-Rock had no idea how J-Mills really felt. He had been acting better than Denziel Washington in Training Day.

"I heard the dude Mo Mo you was trying to get at telling," G-Rock told J-Mills.

It's been so long that J-Mills had stop looking for dude and kind of forgot about it. At any time if he would have caught dude slipping he would have had somebody knock his head off though.

"I aint even know he was locked up," J-Mills said passing G-Rock the dutch.

"Yeah, they caught an indictment out North. He telling on ma manz and them. They said he writing a history book of the whole city for them boys."

"That's one less person I have to worry about killing," J-Mills said while pushing G-Rock in his wheelchair.

G-Rock tried to look back at him and asked, "What you got a hit list?"

"Something like that," J-Mills responded.

G-Rock gave a little scared giggle. It was something about the way J-Mills said it that sent chills throughout his skin.

"I don't understand how these dudes be so tough doing all this dirt but then tell them pigs everything. That's how you know them dudes been bitch all along. On top of that what be really messing me up is people be letting these rats come back to the hood. If I catch any snitch slipping I'm rocking them."

J-Mills hated snitches with a passion. In his squad that was the number one rule (No snitching). They all knew and agreed that if that was broken it was no mercy on whoever, even amongst themselves.

J-Mills and G-Rock had just came out of one of their spots. Parking was always scarce in that area so J-Mills had to push G-Rock a couple of blocks before they got to where they parked at.

"Yo, who told you about that Little Man situation? You knew the details and all big bro." It always bothered J-Mills how G-Rock knew about the Little Man situation. Then for him to deal with him instead said that he couldn't be trusted. That was being disloyal to the dead, all for money. J-Mills would never do one of his boys like that. It would have been a life for a life. All his dudes knew that. He tried to sweet talk G-Rock with that big bro phrase. That wasn't how he talked, he was just trying to get some info out of him.

"I got eyes and ears all over the city. I'm like god in the hood, I see and hear all things," G-Rock said with a smile trying to look back at J-Mills who was pushing him. "You just was talking about you hate snitches. I can't tell you ma sources."

"It's only snitching when you cooperating with the authorities. Plus you supposed to put ya manz up on stuff like that."

J-Mills was trying to get it out of him but it seemed like G-rock wasn't beat. G-Rock had been in the game too long to let somebody pick his brain for some info, his manz or not.

"That's what happened, ma manz put me on point," G-Rock said.

J-Mills was silent for about thirty seconds, contemplating. G-Rock couldn't imagine what was going on in his mind. It always bothered J-Mills. If he knew then somebody else knew and there wasn't any statute of limitations on murder.

"You know dudes don't know how to get in and get out anymore," J-Mills said switching the subject. "That's how dudes be catching indictments or getting bodied. They lose site of the goal and start thinking this shit legal. Especially you old mothafuckas."

G-Rock had never been talked to like that and he knew if he wasn't in that wheelchair that J-Mills wouldn't be calling him that. "I aint old. I'm only thirty four," G-Rock said being proud of his age at the same time feeling like J-Mills was coming at his neck. He couldn't say exactly what he really wanted to say because he felt vulnerable.

"This is a young man's game," J-Mills said with a grin on his face. Of course G-Rock couldn't see it because he had his back to him.

"These young boys don't even know how to wipe their asses right. They don't even like washing their asses let alone getting money. All they want to do is get high and fake wild out on some nut shit. We need dudes like that though, unconscious mothafuckas that don't know when they're getting stunted."

"I guess you got a point. Ya source obviously aint tell you about that other move I had in progress," J-Mills said as they got to the intersection.

"Believe me I know everything I need to know," G-Rock said confidently.

"Alright all hearing all knowing, so you know Parkside mine then? You know this whole time I was taking this shit over little by little and you played right into my hands. You know it was me who shot you and killed Row?" J-Mills was telling him everything.

G-Rock couldn't believe what he was hearing. When he heard him admit to shooting him and Killing Row he stopped the wheelchair right in the middle of the road while cars were coming. The traffic was speeding.

"You know it's going to be me who kill you and fuck Joan, right?" With that said J-Mills pushed G-Rock right in front of an oncoming F-150 that was breaking the speed limit doing about eighty miles an hour. When the truck hit G-rock he went in the air and his wheelchair went flying somewhere else. He landed on his neck. Another car ran him over before coming to a screeching halt. J-Mills didn't stick around to see his crash landing, he just hoped that he was finished.

****

G-Rock's funeral was held at the same place as Row's. A lot of people showed their respects. *They put him back together pretty well* J-Mills thought as he stood there looking at his work. He thought that he was going to be mangled to the point of a closed casket. While standing there J-Mills thought he seen G-Rock get up and start to get out of the casket with the angry face. J-Mills jumped back like he seen a ghost.

"You need to stop attending funerals. This aint ya thing, ya conscious messing with you," Reef said grabbing him and walking him off.

J-Mills had told his boys what had happened at Row's funeral too. They found it funny. "I think you right," J-Mills said. To everybody else it looked like J-Mills was going through something because his manz had just gotten killed. Only if they knew.

Rek was the only one who wasn't fooled. The whole time at the funeral he observed J-Mill's squad. He knew something wasn't right he just couldn't believe it was actually happening. Nobody saw it coming but to him it seemed like the only reasonable answer. He grew up with them, he knew the type of stuff they be on. Out of nowhere the night G-Rock had gotten shot the first time came to mind he had thought he seen J-Mills ride by but wasn't sure. They had his whole hood now so he knew that he had to keep his thoughts to himself.

CHAPTER 36

"Come on Mr. Scott, you supposed to be our eyes and ears out there what's going on?" Lieutenant Lynch wanted to know who was doing all the killing. "That's basically our case," he said closing the folder.

Since Row and G-Rock had gotten killed that set them back to square one in their investigation.

"I told you we should have taken them down when we had the chance," Agent John said. To him dudes from the hood were just like the Pitbull's they loved so much and belong in the cages just like them.

"This was unexpected, at least I never seen it coming," Fat Chop stated. "Nobody in their right mind would go at them."

"That's the problem, nobody in them streets are in their right minds," Agent John said.

Fat Chop heard the racial under tone coming from Agent John, he chose to ignore him. He felt like he could talk to Fat Chop how he wanted because to him he was nothing but a piece of shit snitch who was just like the rest of them.

"They did so much dirt in them streets it's hard to know where the hit came from but if you ask me I think it's something going on inside Parkside that we don't know about." Fat Chop knew things weren't adding up.

"With them two dead whose running the show now, because things seem like they're still the same out there," Agent Cano said?

"I'm not sure but I think it's this guy," Fat Chop said pointing to J-Mills picture on the wall. "This could possibly be all his work."

"What we got you for if you aint never sure about anything," Agent John asked?

"These dudes know how to move. They young but they aint dumb," Fat Chop said.

"Alright, get close to him then," Lieutenant Lynch said.

"It's not that easy, every time I'm around him I be getting these crazy vibes like he don't like me."

"I don't like you either, do you get them vibes around me?"

Fat Chop just looked at Agent John when he said that and kept talking. "It's hard to read him so I speak and keep it moving. We got Ashley working on his friend Mir. I'm fly with him too so I'ma try to work him one way and she's going to continue to work him the other way."

"That sound gay," Agent John said laughing. He liked messing with Fat Chop. He really didn't have any respect for him because he was a snitch. He knew he was a bitch. No police really liked snitches, they just made their jobs easier. They had their own codes and one of them was no snitching because they did a lot of dirt themselves so why would they like a snitch that was telling on his own peoples.

****

"What's good my guy," Fat Chop asked Mir being extra jolly?

"Who this," Mir asked?

"It's Chop." Fat Chop never called himself or even introduced himself as Fat Chop unless he had to.

"Oh, I aint recognize the number. What's good, what you got a new number?"

"Nah, this ma little chick phone. I need to talk you. I got an emergency going on."

"I bet you do," Mir responded knowing what he was getting at."

"When you free?"

"Get at me later, around seven."

Later that day Fat Chop came through and scooped Mir.

"How Ashley doing," Fat Chop asked as if he didn't know.

"She good, she be staying with me now."

"That's what's up, take good care of her. She good peoples for real."

"You already know."

"I need you to come through for me, things aint been looking good for me."

"Yeah, what you need," Mir asked?

"I need five of them. What's the numbers?"

"For you, 30,000. Only because you ma dude."

"Good looking, that's some real shit."

"Just for now on get at me. Drop me off at my car and give me about a half, I'll give you a call.

Little did Mir know that their whole conversation was being recorded. The objective was to get to J-Mills but the way Mir took that order the Feds no longer thought that J-Mills was the head of things. They figured Mir was running the show now and they was about to get him exactly where they wanted him.

Fat Chop received the call and met Mir on Langham and walnut. The feds was listening and watching everything. They now had more than enough to put Mir away for a long time but the feds never wanted one individual, they wanted him and whoever was connected to him.

CHAPTER 37

Mir gave his mother a hug and a kiss as he entered the house. He adored his mother, his father also. Growing up he had them both which was a rare thing in Camden. It was also a shame because without a father figure who cared or gave their kids the attention they wanted they looked for it in other dudes and more than likely it was going to be a hustler trying to manipulate them.

Mir was the only child, both of his parents had good jobs. He didn't need to sell drugs when he was younger but they messed up raising him in Camden. Dope and coke boys ran Camden so that's what so many youngens aspired to be. Since his parents' divorce he only seen his father once in a while. When he was young his father was always busy and he was running the streets, now he was always busy too.

Paul seemed to be doing a good job taking his father's spot. He kept his mother happy and that's all Mir wanted. Paul sat in the chair that would have only been reserved for Mir's father. He read the newspaper like a true old head. After Mir got done chatting with his mom him and Paul got a chance to talk.

Mir was telling Paul to get ready for him because he was about to start coming for much more than the ten bricks he was getting from him. J-Mills was about to go in and he wanted to introduce him to Anwar. The dilemma was that Anwar didn't want to deal with anybody but J-Mills. So J-Mills was trying to set up a delivery and pick up system so they could keep things moving. He didn't want things to fall apart while he was gone. Mir had his own plans though.

CHAPTER 38

Isha came out of the house and was about to get in her car when she looked up the block she seen someone standing under this tree watching her on some Michael Myers stuff. It was too dark for her to see who it was or even if it was a male or female. She reached in her purse and grabbed her 380 and began walking towards the person. Whoever it was took off running. She got in her car with the intentions of chasing the person down. She pulled off fast, got to the corner and tried to slow down but the brakes was out. She tried the emergency brake but it didn't work. She turned right and ran on the curb unto the side of a house.

J-Mills came rushing in the emergency room. Isha was patched up with minor cuts and bruises. She was happy to see him. She hugged him and cried, he held her and promised her that they were out of that house. It was no going back and he meant it this time. She told him about everything and they found out that someone had cut the brake lines.

J-Mills couldn't figure out who would want to harm his lady. He vowed to body whoever it was. He knew if dudes couldn't get to you that they'll get to someone close to you, but to him this was some bitch shit. Cutting brake lines, who did that?

They stayed at a hotel until they found another place to live. All the houses J-Mills owned were in the hood. They eventually found something nice to rent in Cherry Hill, a suburban outskirt gated community on the low.

****

Time was ticking for J-Mills. He had to go in and do a county bid, a 364 for the gun charge he caught the night he got shot. The last couple of years he been postponing his court dates but they wasn't letting him do it anymore so he was tightening up, getting ready to go sit down for a year.

J-Mills put Mir in charge of everything. Pooh and Reef would make sure he got his cut. Everybody was the overseer of everybody, that way it wasn't any big I's or little U's. Nothing was to change, Mir was just making sure the work landed and got distributed right.

The way J-Mills saw it was he could use a vacation. Years of running could be tiresome. The only thing he was worried about was things falling apart. He only had to do a year but he knew a lot could change in that year.

About a week before he had to go in he received a call from Angie claiming that she was pregnant. He didn't want to believe her but he had to face the fact he was hitting it raw and he wasn't pulling out every time.

"You sure it's mind," he asked nice and calm trying not to offend her? The question itself was offensive to a faithful woman. Only the unfaithful pretended to be offended.

"Of course it is. I don't be laying down with more than one person, I'm not no dirty chick."

"I'm saying, you know I got a girl."

"I aint killing ma baby," Angie said letting him know in case he was thinking about an abortion. "I'll take care of it myself if it came down to it."

"Come on now Angie, this me you talking to. You know I aint one of them nut ass dudes. I'ma be there and take care of mine."

Due to his religion J-Mills didn't believe in abortions. Her getting one wasn't a thought of his. He just always pictured him and Isha having kids together. He started telling Angie how he was about to go in and do a county bid. She let him know that she was definitely going to ride out with him.

The whole next week was a big party for J-Mills. He spent it clubbing, getting drunk, smutting broads, and having fun. One night they were in a local spot downtown called Camden Art Yard. It was a nice little outdoors spot that drew a lot of outskirt people. Even though it was in the hood it wasn't as hood as the rest of the local bars. Probably because if you wanted to order something to eat or drink the only way you could pay was with a debit or credit card.

"J-Mills J-Mills, what's good brah," Fly said as he walked up.

J-Mills had quite a few dudes around him but for the most part everybody he came there with was mingling. Him and fly shook hands and embraced each other.

"I been trying to get up with you. I got something to tell you but you be on the move."

"You know how it is," J-Mills said as they walked to the bar.

"Yeah, you out here getting it."

"I aint the only one, you know I know how ya'll eating." Fly was still getting money with Meek. Over the years he had stepped his game up. "You still got something to tell me," J-Mills asked curiously?

"Yeah, look you know how our relationship is. We don't have to get money together or be around each other for you to know I see you as ma bro and wouldn't stir you wrong." The whole time J-Mills was nodding his head yeah in agreement. "I know Rek supposed to be ya manz but I heard he the one who got you shot by running his mouth to Bush about you killing his cousin. I don't know if you knew but Little Man was Bush's manz."

J-Mills looked around to make sure nobody else heard what Fly had told him. "Good looking bro, I appreciate you putting me on point."

"It's only right, I know you would do the same for me. Ma source reliable too."

"If it came from you I'm going with it. I don't think you'll deliver just anything to me." J-Mills definitely could see that being true about Rek. Their friendship wasn't how it used to be since he did that to Rek's cousin.

Reef had ordered some shots of 151 and brung it over to J-Mills and Fly who were now standing near a table. "Don't ask no questions just throw them back. This some old head shit I'm putting ya'll up on," Reef said.

J-Mills looked at it, smelt it, and without any questions said, "I trust you with ma life so I'ma see what this is about." He gulped down the shot and it hit his chest unlike anything he ever had before. He started coughing and trying to catch his breath at the same time. Mir and Pooh was laughing at him. Fly had put his drink on the table, he didn't want any parts of that. Some chick who was standing buy began patting J-Mills on the back.

"You alright," she asked?

J-Mills was bent over still coughing. The chick gave him her corona to chase it down with.

"Good looking," he said wiping tears from his eyes. When he looked she was all up on him. Her face was alright but her body was crazy. She was thick thick with a flat stomach. She had on a grey netted see through one piece with nothing on under it. Her ass and titties were just there. Surprisingly, everything sat right because she looked a little order. *Dam* J-Mills thought as he recovered his sight back. Now he was checking her out. She stood over him like she was really concerned.

"I feel like you saved ma life," he said joking. All his dudes started laughing. "Don't pay them any mind. Have a seat," he told her.

J-Mills started ordering her drinks. She must have known she was going to be drinking all night for free because as J-Mills was talking to her he noticed that she didn't have any pockets nor did he see a purse in her hand so she couldn't of had any money on her. Her name was Stephanie but to him her name was irrelevant. The only thing she said that stuck with him was when she said she was leaving with him.

Out of nowhere Nina showed up and was talking to Reef. Whenever J-Mills and his peoples went out they drew a lot of attention because of how they moved, what they pulled up in and how they spent. Tonight the real attention was on Stephanie who was basically walking around naked like it was nothing. She wasn't one of them chicks that be sitting still either. She was real live entertainment, dancing, taking pictures, and moving around freely.

When J-Mills was ready to leave she was right there on his arm. All J-Mills dudes left following him except Reef, he stayed back with Nina. Stephanie got into the back of the Cadillac truck, Pooh rode shotgun. Mir, Taj, and Sha was celebrating with J-Mills since he was about to go in. They had got some ladies of their own out of the Camden Art Yard.

They all went to the Holiday Inn and got separate rooms except J-Mills, Pooh, and Stephanie. As soon as they got in the room Stephanie went to the bathroom. She came back out with nothing on. What she was wearing was now in her hand. She placed it on the dresser. J-Mills started taking pictures of her with his phone. She was posing like she was in a porn magazine, opening her pussy, putting a finger in her mouth and showing them all the positions they could possibly have her in. All that did was turn them on more. After he took enough pictures they ran a train on her.

About an hour later while they were chilling Mir knocked on the door, J-Mills opened the door for him. "It smell like all ass in here," Mir joked as he walked in. He seen Stephanie thick ass laying there and wanted some.

"You might as well tell ya peoples to come in here and chill," J-Mills told Mir. He wanted to see who Mir had and how she was on it. That old saying from Snoop Dog (Aint no fun if ma homies can't have none) was true amongst them, unless it was one of their main chicks or wifies. Everything else was fun and games.

CHAPTER 39

The next couple of days J-Mills spent putting quality time in with his lady. That Friday he went in, was processed and sent to seven day lock up. As soon as he went in there was already four dudes boxed in this little room. There was only two beds. The only place for him to put his mat was a little space near the toilet. Either his head was going to be near the toilet or under the bed, that's how closed in everything was. *Aint no way I'm sleeping on this nasty ass floor,* he thought to himself. He tapped dude who had the bottom bunk. Dude was curled up in the fiddle position with the covers over his head. When J-Mills tapped him he peeked his head from under the covers.

"Get up, you know what it is."

"What, you better get the fuck outta here," dude said before putting the covers back over his head.

J-Mills grabbed him by the ankles, drug him off the bunk and stumped him out. After beating dude into submission while the others watched he threw dude mat on the floor then put his on the bunk and made it up nice and neat like he was in the military before.

In Camden County everyone got sent to seven day lock up from the door. It was so many people coming in there that J-Mills only stayed for three days before he went to population. He was sent to 5 north A. Mostly everybody there he either knew, seen around or they knew him or heard of him. That's how small the city was. In population they didn't place you in a room they just opened the gate for you and let you find ya own way. When somebody new came to the tier everyone stood around waiting to see who it was. For a lot of dudes when that gate opened it was like feeding them to the sharks. They might have enemies on that tier or just wasn't built for that type of environment.

J-Mills didn't have them type of problems. His peoples directed him to what room to put his stuff in. They gave him food, cosmetics and let him know what was theirs was his. Little Chris offered his bottom bunk. J-Mills humbly denied it. It was a difference, these was his peoples. If they wasn't he would of fought for it. It was an egotistical, pride, testosterone, respect thing when it came to them bunks and them floors in the county. Little Chris insisted saying that he wouldn't feel right with J-Mills on the floor while he was on the bunk. J-Mills respected that and accepted his offer. He knew his position and couldn't downplay it if he wanted to. At the same time Little Chris knew by being a good dude it would come back to him ten folds.

Fu and Tone were the other two in the room with them. They had got caught in a raid on Haddon. Little Chris was locked up for a shooting. J-Mills took this opportunity to instill all qualities in them that real dudes should possess. The number one rule which was already known was no snitching but through their conversations he made sure to always put emphasis on it. He also harped on loyalty and discipline. In that cell they had deep conversations about things that was going on. J-Mills got their perspective and input but he could only tell them but so much. It was levels and they knew and respected it but when he talked they held on to every word like he was the second coming of Christ.

J-Mills made sure all his dudes were taking care of. Lawyers if they didn't have one. They jailed different when he came on the tier. Wasn't any of that goofy stuff going on. They read books, played chest, worked out, got their hands sharp, went to the law library to work on their cases, watched sports, and politicked on getting money. J-Mills was getting them right how he had things on the streets and was teaching them the importance of keeping the Family tight.

Isha and Angie was making their regular visits. He made sure they didn't bump heads. One day Isha missed a visit so he called home. When she picked up he could tell something was wrong.

"Hello."

"What's up baby, you good? I missed you today."

"I know I tried to make it but I really wasn't feeling good. I had threw up."

"Are you alright? Did you eat some bad food," J-Mills asked being concerned?

"I don't know, I got an appointment to see the doctors tomorrow."

That Wednesday when Isha came to visit she had a Kool Aid smile on her face. She was always happy to see her boo but today she was extra with it. She had been holding back something so she could deliver it in person.

"I got some good news," she said as soon as he picked up the phone.

In the county there was no contact visits only window visits. Usually J-Mills kept his poker face on, no emotions and real nonchalant but Isha was his sweet spot. Plus she played so much that he couldn't be on his gorilla shit when she was around. Just seeing her smile made him smile.

"What's this good news," J-Mills asked?

"We're having a baby," Isha said excited.

J-Mills heart floodered with joy. Something it didn't do when Angie told him she was pregnant. He might have been happier than Isha, he was just too gangsta to be all extra.

"For real, dam. I got to get out there to you and ma baby. I need to be there to rub ya stomach and do all that good stuff."

"I know right. You going to be home soon baby, don't worry we're going to do this together. The doctor said I'm eight weeks and you almost got two months in so the baby a be about three months when you get home."

After that visit J-Mills whole perspective on life began to change. He always dreamed of starting his own family because he really didn't have one growing up. He would watch T.V. shows like My Wife and Kids and imagine what it would be like to have a beautiful family like that. Before he got that news from Isha he was doing his bid like nothing. It was only feeling like a time out for him but now that he knew that he was going to miss his child being born it was feeling like a stretch.

He took it as motivation. Them twenty pull ups turned into thirties, them fifty pushups turned into a hundred. He had stopped smoking, all he was doing was getting focused. He knew he would eventually have to let Isha know about Angie and the baby she was having but he wasn't sure how that was going to go. He definitely wasn't going to tell her while he was locked up.

He thought about marrying Isha and falling back from the game. Not giving it up but just handling the shipments from Anwar and him and Mir splitting the profits 50/50 how him and G-Rock was doing after Row was dead. J-Mills felt that if Mir could hold it down while he was locked up then that was something that was going to happen. He knew Mir always wanted to be that dude anyway. J-Mills didn't have any problems splitting the profits with his guys. He wasn't greedy. He just had to get G-Rock and Row out the way so his squad could control things.

CHAPTER 40

"Yo," Mir said answering his phone sounding like he was half sleep.

"What's good playa? I'm ready for you again," Fat Chop said.

Mir looked at his watch and seen that it was almost 1:00pm. He stayed out late and was hung over. He knew that he had a move to make with Paul soon so he got up.

"Nah, not right now. I gotta make a move but I'll get at you tonight." Mir told Fat chop.

"Like what time playa," Fat Chop asked trying to get specifics?

"Before ten, I'ma call you though."

"Alright, be easy," Fat Chop said before hanging up. Their whole conversation was being recorded as usual. The feds had Mir tailed so they could find out about this move he said he had to make.

A few hours later Mir met with Paul. Paul was sitting in a Blue Expedition. Mir parked his car across the street and got in the truck with him. They talked for a while then Paul got out of the truck and got in Mir's car. To the feds that was a clear transaction even though they didn't see any product exchange hands. They still didn't run down though.

They followed Mir to a house where he unloaded a few bags. He stayed in the house for about an hour then came out with just one bag. Not long after he met up with Fat Chop giving him the bag they seen him come back out of the house with. The evidence on Mir kept piling up. It was too easy to lock him up. He was moving as though what he was doing was legal.

Seeing that Paul was the connect they started tailing him. They found out who he was and ran his name. He only had minor run ins with the law when he was young, nothing serious. They did a full background check on the cars he drove and the house he lived in. Nothing was in his name, he never paid taxes, didn't have any credit cards, as far as they knew he didn't have a driver license but he lived in a five hundred thousand dollar house that was in his wife name. Everything they owned was in her name. The feds knew she couldn't have acquired all that by herself because when she did work she worked in an old folks home and they wasn't paying enough for her to come up like that. Mir's mom didn't know Paul was married. She had no idea she was a jump off. Paul brought about another investigation. He was a big fish who they weren't going to let off the hook.

CHAPTER 41

Angie never skipped a beat when it came to her weekly visits. She was actually riding like she said she would. Over the months J-Mills had watched her stomach get bigger and bigger. Even though he hoped she wasn't pregnant in the beginning when he seen she was and how happy she was to be having his child he knew he had to be a father to his child. It was no way he was going to neglect his responsibility and be a dead beat dad. He never had respect for dudes that didn't take care of their kids. The way he seen it if dudes couldn't be loyal to their kids then it was no way they could be loyal to him. He never let them kind of dudes get too close, they get used for what they were worth which wasn't much.

Angie was one of them chicks that knew almost everything that went on in the city. All her friends did was gossip. Her friends would be in that salon spreading everybody's business. J-Mills had been told Angie to keep his name out of her mouth. He even explained to her why since chicks be acting like they don't be understanding that's how they be getting dudes robbed and killed. At the same time he drained her for info. Especially while he was locked up. She put him up on more stuff going on in the city than any of his dudes did.

Every visit day Angie would come the hour after Isha would leave. She knew who Isha was but they never talked, not even in the salon. Isha had no idea she was messing with her man on the low. Twice a week she would see Isha leaving and noticed that her stomach was getting bigger also. This made Angie furious, it added fuel to her jealous fire.

By being pregnant she figured she had one up on Isha but if Isha was pregnant too that wouldn't be the case. She knew J-Mills loved Isha more than her and couldn't allow her to lock him down with a baby. In her mind the baby she was having was going to allow J-Mills and her to spend more time together so she could eventually win him over. Angie was due to have her baby soon and vowed that when she dropped her load she would make sure she completed what she had been trying to do.

CHAPTER 42

Paul sat in the restaurant with one of his shooters, another old head like himself. They sat near the window in clear view of the truck station across the street. Every month they made this trip to Arizona. It wasn't long before the truck they had been waiting for pulled up to the station. His driver switched trucks with the other driver then pulled off. A van of shooters he employed to protect his shipment drove behind them.

Another ten minutes or so after the transaction Paul and his shooter headed to the airport. They never followed the truck, they would only see that it got in the right hands and trust them to drive it to Camden. Paul could have hired someone to be there but it was way too much money involved and he was in the habit of doing it himself.

Five hours later Paul and his shooter landed at The Philadelphia International Airport. After they made it through TSA security check two white men in suites approached them and asked them to step in a room. Paul was scared to death. The scenarios going through his mind was endless. In all of them he seen himself in prison. *I'm too old for this shit* he thought. Airport security had tightened up a lot because of the things that were going on around the world but Paul knew that this didn't have anything to do with any of that. He had a gut feeling that his run had come to an end. They were placed in separate rooms. Paul silently kept praying that they hadn't ran down on his shipment.

Paul sat in that room for an hour sweating. The feds stood on the other side of the two way mirror watching him stress. After they felt like they made him sweat enough Agent Cain walked in with two cups of Dunkin Donuts coffee. He pulled up a chair, slid a cup of coffee to Paul, pulled out a cigar and offered one to Paul.

168

"I'm good, them things take years off of ya life," Paul said.

Agent Cain smiled as he lit his cigar anyway. "Why would you want to live a long life when you're going to be spending the rest of it in prison?"

That wasn't sarcasm, he was being facetious and Paul knew by the way he was coming at him that it was over. Agent Cain knew no matter what that he had Paul and that it was only one way he wouldn't spend the rest of his life in prison and that was if he cooperated with him.

"Look, I'ma cut the bullshit guy. I got you by the balls. We got everything. We didn't even have to pitch that old ass driver for him to start screaming your name. He didn't want to spend the rest of his life behind bars and you're older than him so I know you don't. You know how this thing work, one hand wash the other. What can you tell us that can help you? Before you start saying anything remember that your life is in your own hands. Think about your family."

In came another Agent who fixed a video recorder on a tripod and faced it towards Paul. He didn't pay them any mind. After he set it up and turned it on he left the room.

Paul watched him the whole time. Once he left Paul put is head down in defeat. He sold drugs his whole life and never did a bid. Now he was caught with the motherload.

Thick smoke from Agent Cain's cigar lit up the room. He sat looking at Paul patiently waiting. For him, It wasn't a question if he was going to break or not, the question was when. He wanted the pleasure of breaking him, that's why he kept saying things that made him conscious of everything at stake.

When Paul lifted his head up he started singing. He hit that high note like the old Whitney Houston before crack had messed up her vocals. He started snitching on dudes from state to state and one of them was Mir.

CHAPTER 43

Mir had come home early after receiving a call from Ashley sounding like she was fiending for him to dick her down. Bout time they hung up he was there. She opened the door wearing this sexy see through lingerie. He instantly became aroused. They kissed and she lead him upstairs. As Mir looked at her ass from the back all he could think of was the things he was going to do to her body. When they got in the room Mir started coming out of his clothes.

"What you think you doing with them," he asked Ashley as she pulled out some hand cuffs? The kind she had in hand wasn't even the play kind with the fur on them. These were real, the ones you really needed a cop key in order to get them off. Mir wasn't thinking about that though.

"Come on babe please? Remember you told me you was going to let me do it one day? You're going to love it."

Mir was hesitant at first but he eventually agreed to play the submission roll.

"Don't try to put anything in ma butt, I aint with none of that."

"I'm not silly," she said and started to tie one of her scarfs around his eyes then she kissed him. She had him lay down and hand cuffed both hands to the headboard and tied his legs to the bottom poles. "I'll be right back baby," she said and kissed his lips one last time.

Naked and blind folded all negative thoughts was going through his mind but he couldn't imagine what was really going on. This was something that at one point or another in every dude life

171

they said that they would never do, not because they wasn't with the freaky stuff but because they didn't want to be vulnerable.

"It's getting chilly Ashley, ma man going to start shrinking. I don't even know why you got me blind folded, you know I'm a visual person. I gotta see that body in motion while we getting it in."

The whole time he was talking she didn't hear any of it. She had put on her clothes, went downstairs and opened the door for them boys. They came in eleven deep. When they got upstairs Mir was still talking.

"Ashley, is that you baby?"

"It's me baby," one of the male agents said in his fake female voice before taking the blind fold off of Mir's face.

"What the fuck," Mir said shocked!

The agents had their weapons drawn on him. Mir looked around the room and his eyes landed on Ashley. There was disbelief and confusion on his face. She dropped her head not wanting to look at him. Another one of the agents started reading him his charges and memorandum rights.

"Bitch you set me up. You stupid bitch, I gave you everything."

He was cursing her out. The only thing he could move was his head. They uncuffed him from the bed and cuffed his hands behind his back, put some clothes on him and took him out.

Nobody knew Mir had got locked up. The only call he made was to his mother. He told her all about the situation with Paul and the feds was listening in on every word. She was shocked to find out that Paul was a drug lord.

CHAPTER 44

Pooh found out the next day from some chick name Carla he was messing with that knew Mir. She had seen the paper and called Pooh.

"His chick acting like she don't want to pick up the phone. I been calling all day."

"Mir girl," Reef asked Pooh? "Man she probably took everything and spined off on him. You know how it go when dudes catch charges, everybody start spinning off. Try to call his mom. She might know what's going on."

"I don't have that number."

"Let's go see her."

"I think it's best we stay away because they might be looking for us too."

Pooh and Reef had enough coke for a couple of weeks but they didn't know the connect. They really couldn't go to other people because they were the plugs for a lot of local dudes. Instead of selling the coke they had for wholesale they put it all on the blocks out Parkside so their dudes could eat while they figured things out.

Reef and Pooh got low fast, they didn't know if they were next or what. Within a month they ran through everything they had. In the process of moving what they had they started dealing with Mack. Mack was heavy in the game. He had his own connects but they had better prices so Mack started dealing with them. Now he was serving them.

Mack couldn't really fill the order but he was helpful. A couple other dudes came through but they wasn't trying to deal with everybody. The goal was to get things together but it was slowly falling apart.

A couple months went by before Pooh received a phone call from Mir.

"Hello," Pooh said answering his phone. It was nine in the morning. Pooh was laid up with one of his shorties. Pooh accepted the collect call. They had Mir in FDC in Philly.

"What's good bro," Mir said?

"Mir was trying to sound like everything was good but Pooh knew him. He could hear that something was wrong. He was nervous himself answering the phone for Mir. He was still his dude so he didn't want to not pick up when he knew his dude needed him the most.

"What's good ma boy, how you holding up?"

"They trying to burn ya boy," Mir said.

"What they talking about?"

"They talking life. Even the deal they coming at me with is 30 years."

"Dam bro, I don't know what to say. What can I do? You know if you need anything let me know."

"I do need you to do something for me. I need you to go to Samara's house and get them bricks of coke, take them to ma peoples. He going to be at Applebee's parking lot in a Blue Expedition. Give him the bricks and he going to give you the money and take the money to my mom. She'll know what to do with it."

Pooh sat and listened as Mir went on talking reckless saying things that he wouldn't have said on the phone if he was home. One of their rules was to keep it phone friendly. He let him talk then he began acting like he didn't know what he was talking about because he knew them boys must have broken him and that Mir was trying to set him up. *This mothafucka must think I'm stupid* Pooh thought to himself with a broken heart. It was always a sad day when the feds broke what was supposed to be a real one.

"Bro you know I aint into that life. I can't get caught up in that. Have a nice life playa." Click!

Pooh dropped his phone on the ground knowing he was going to trash it. He grabbed his other phone and immediately called Reef and put him on things.

"Yo bro, if Mir call you do not answer. Them boys broke him. He just tried to set me up."

"Dam for real, what he say?"

"I can't even tell you that shit on the phone but he a done deal. He talking, be on point."

Pooh switched all his numbers and moved. He told Reef to do the same, but Reef didn't want to really believe that Mir was going out like that. He figured Pooh was paranoid.

****

The feds ran in the trap house they had out Pollock on Jackson. They didn't find anything. Pooh had moved the location to another spot.

Reef was coming home after a long day in the hood. His house was about seven houses from the corner, he was riding up the street leading to his block when he seen all these unmarked cop cars on the block looking like they was in front of his house. As he got closer he slowed down enough to see if it was his house or not. Then he seen one of the DEA agents come out of his house with the metal thing they used to knock down the door. Reef rode by trying to look without looking so they wouldn't see his face.

"Yo bro," Reef said once Pooh picked up his phone. "Yeah he told them boys something."

"I told you. What made you say that though?"

"They all in ma crib. Meet me at Forest Hill."

"Alright, I'm there."

It was around 11:15pm when Pooh and Reef met up. They both parked their cars in the back of Park Blvd houses and walked to the park so they wouldn't drawl any attention. Reef was posted on the sliding board smoking weed when Pooh walked up.

"You getting high at a time like this?"

"This is what got me calm," Reef said passing Pooh the dutch. "I called you here because we gotta figure out what's next."

"I don't know," Pooh responded as nervous as Reef. He knew that if they ran down in Reef's spot then they had ran down in his old spot too but he had abandon ship. He abandoned every spot he knew Mir had knew anything about.

"What did you have in ya house," Pooh asked?

"I aint have no coke or anything. I had a gun and some money, oh and some haze. If he telling it's going to be bigger than that. He probably telling about bodies and everything."

"Yeah right," Pooh said as he took another pull of the haze then passed it. "Go get all the money you got and be out. This is where we go our separate ways. Fuck all the money dudes owe us, it's over with. I hope you don't have ya money in none of them spots Mir knew about because if you do you can forget that too. They waiting for us to back track. They used to dumb dudes doing shit like that. Fuck everything and everybody, just go!"

The whole time Reef was looking at the ground thinking then he shook his head no as soon as he thought he was certain. "Nah, he don't know about the spots I keep ma dough at."

"You going to have to leave ya chick too bro. They going to be all over her hoping she lead them to you."

"Yeah you right. I love you bro," Reef said and they shook hands and embraced each other.

"I love you too bro, real shit. No matter how ugly it get you know the number one rule right," Pooh asked?

"You already know bro, you don't ever have to worry about me snitching. I'm taking mine to the grave."

With that said they walked to their cars. Reef sat in his car contemplating his next move. He watched Pooh pull off. At that point he didn't want to pull off because they might know the car he was driving. He picked up the phone and called Nina.

"Hello."

"Yo come get me. I'm in the back of Forest Hill in ma car."

"What's wrong, are you ok?"

"Just come get me, I'll tell you when you get here."

Reef started champing a Black and Mild. Nina showed up about twenty minutes later and they went to her house. As soon as Reef got there he went to her room and got his money. He had

177

started messing with Nina on the regular after Pooh told him how Mir was talking on the phone. He had made her house one of his spots.

"What's wrong," Nina asked coming in the room? He was stuffing money into the bookbag."

"I gotta go on the run."

"For what," she asked in a concerned voice?

The way he looked at her let her know that she just asked a stupid question. She knew his occupation. He still answered her question.

"The feds looking for me. They was in ma house earlier. This pussy telling."

"Who?"

"Mir."

"You can stay here. They'll never find you here. Don't nobody really know we mess around."

When Reef got done putting the money in the bag he sat on the edge of the bed thinking about what she said. He needed her while he was on the run but staying there was something else, he knew he really had to get out of the city. Meanwhile he chose to stay there until he figured things out.

The next day Nina handed Reef the Courier Post New Paper. The raid made front page of the South Jersey News section. Reef and Pooh's faces was in there under wanted. They also had a lot of others in there but nothing about J-Mills. In the paper they talked about the bust on Paul, the investigation of Mir and the things they retrieved from Reef's house. Reef wasn't stressed or worried.

Everything seemed surreal to him. It was nothing he could do but he wasn't going to turn himself in. If the feds wanted him then they would have to catch him.

Two months had passed since Reef been on the run and he haven't been outside once. All he did was look out the window from time to time. He wasn't taking any chances, he didn't want anybody seeing him but lately he been feeling like he needed some fresh air. Nina was more than happy to have him there. She was acting like they were married, cooking dinner every night. Anything he needed he just sent her to get. She was more than willing to do anything he asked.

They were having sex every day, two to three times most days. He never had sex with one female so much in his life, not even his girl. He was always in something different. He probably appreciated her more than any dude has ever especially since he knew if he got caught he was going to be without pussy for a very long time. Seeing Nina walk around all day half naked had him on some animal stuff.

Nina had really stop going out with her friends how she used to. She went to work, shopping, or to a relative house back home. She was loving having a man all to herself and he was making sure she was good and didn't need for anything.

It was a stormy Thursday in May, still about 70 degrees out but Reef had become restless. Working out in the house wasn't doing it anymore. His body needed to stretch out beyond the house. He figured that it was a perfect day to venture out since people barely be out in harsh weather like that. Nina tried to convince him not to go.

"What you going out for it's raining?"

"That's exactly why I'm going out, aint nobody going to be out. I'm going to go chill for a little. I'm going to be good, aint nothing going to happen."

He tried to assure her that he'll be right back. She tried everything in her power to keep him from going. She was in front of the door in her bra and panties while he was trying to leave.

"I got a bad feeling. You know the city always hot."

"I'm coming right back," he said trying to open the door.

"I'm horny," she said and began hugging, kissing, and grabbing on his dick. She felt him get hard and knew she had him. She tried leading him away from the door. He pulled her panties down right there and bent her over. Five minutes of going hard he bust off all in her. He got up, pulled his pants up, put his hood on his head, smiled at her mad face, opened the door and left.

It was around 9:30 at night. The streets looked empty. The rain was coming down hard. Only a few cars were on the road. This was one of them days hood dudes were supposed to take off, go in the house and put some quality time in with their lady. He rode through every part of the city how him and his boys used to when they were young and first started having cars. It brought back memories. He also felt a sense of peace as he thought and rode around without any music, only the sound of the rain pouring down.

A car was coming down Park Blvd, they were crossing paths. Reef seen the car but didn't really pay it any mind until it started flickering the lights and beeping the horn. Reef looked in his rearview mirror but didn't stop. He knew that whoever it was wanted to get Nina's attention not his because he had her car. Reef turned up Haddon headed towards midtown. The car had made a

U-turn got behind Reef and started high beaming him down. He didn't want to pull over but the person behind the wheel was persistent. Finally he pulled over and the car pulled next to him. The rain was preventing a clear view. They both rolled down their windows at the same time shocking one another. The look they gave each other was awkward. Reef was kind of relieved, he had no idea that he shouldn't have been.

"O shit, what's good bro," Fat Chop said like he was shocked in a good way?

"What's up money?"

"I'm about to pull over."

Fat Chop pulled over and got in the car with Reef. They were parked on Haddon in front of the Salvation Army.

"It's good to see you," Fat Chop lied as he got in the car. "What's good, how you been holding up?"

"I'm good just laying low."

"I see. I was out here creeping. I thought you was Nina, thought I had some pussy for the night."

Reef felt a little way about that comment. He was having way too much sex with Nina not to have any emotions for her. At the same time he knew her history so it was what it was.

"I know things might be hard for you on the run but if you need me for anything I'm here. I got a couple spots in other states you can get low at. The best thing is to get away from here and stay away."

Fat Chop acted like he sincerely wanted to help but he was really trying to lay a trap.

"I'm good right now, I'll hit you if I need you though, thanks."

"What's up with Pooh?"

"I don't know, we might not ever see each other again. Shit was good while it lasted though."

"Things messed up ever since ya'll left, you see it haven't been anybody out. If ya'll still was active dudes a be swimming in this shit trying to trap. I'm still doing what I do but I be laying low. It's not the same."

Not knowing that Fat Chop was working with the feds Mir had tried to snitch on him too, of course that one didn't go through. After about a half an hour talk they went their separate ways. Reef went back to Nina's house.

Fat Chop felt like a cop that had finally found his suspect. It was no doubt in his mind that that was Nina's car Reef was driving. He'd been in it enough times to know when he seen it. The feds had been looking all over for Reef and Pooh. Fat Chop waited to about 1:30am and rode by Nina's house to confirm is theory. There it was in front of her house like he thought, the exact same license plates.

The next day Reef was sitting on the couch in his boxers watching the big Samsung flat screen. Nina was in the kitchen doing something. The feds kicked in the door and scared the life out of Reef. He jumped up, grabbed the AK that was standing against the wall and ran up the steps. He looked down from the top of the steps, two agents was trying to come up behind him. He let them have it, letting off at least twelve shots. They fell down the steps. A few shots was fired back at him.

"It's the police, come out with your hands up."

Reef heard them announce it late. He probably just killed two agents. Surrendering wasn't an option. His mind and heart was racing thinking about an escape route. The only way out was to bang out and he knew it.

"Fuck," he said real low. He never seen himself going out like this. The circumstance wasn't in his control. He stood at the side of the top of the steps with his back against the wall and the AK pointed upward. He heard the steps start to squeak. He poked the gun around the corner of the wall and started shooting down the steps dropping another agent who stupidly tried to creep up the steps. He ran to the back room window and didn't see anybody. He began to climb out that's when it seem like they all came out of nowhere. They were in the back yard with their guns pointed up at him. He was still in the window. One leg still in the house with most of his body out. He knew it was over, he wasn't going alive. He tried to lift his gun up, before he could do any of that he was hit with a head shot followed by others that ripped through his body.

CHAPTER 45

For the last couple of months Isha had been staying at her mother's house. It was convenient for her commute to the county to see J-Mills. Plus she was almost due. The last thing she wanted to do was get caught in that Cherry Hill traffic while in labor.

Angie had her baby two months ago. She was proud to be a mother and even more proud that J-Mills was the baby's father. They had gotten a DNA test and it came back 99.9% his. She gave birth to a handsome baby boy that looked just like J-Mills. One look at the baby and J-Mill's knew it was his, he still had to get that test because he knew a couple situations where dudes were claiming kids that wasn't theirs. He refused to get played like that. One thing he hadn't figured out yet was how to break the news to Isha. He knew he couldn't hide it forever, he also knew he couldn't tell her while he was locked up.

Isha had left her purse in the car. She came out the house and got it. While shutting the door she never got a chance to see Angie walk up with a bat. She hit Isha right on top of the head knocking her to the ground. Isha looked up from the ground dazed as she caught another blow. Isha made a hurtful noise. She was on her back like a turtle trying to block the blows from the bat but Angie was getting them in there in the open spots.

"Please no, I'm pregnant," Isha pleaded for her life and the life of her unborn child. She was screaming as loud as she could in hopes of someone coming out there to save her. No one came. Angie swung that bat like a maniac. Eventually there was nothing Isha could do but ball up.

****

J-Mills was in the county going through it. He knew that he could possibly be getting indicted soon. It was nothing he could do but pray, wish, and hope Mir left him out for whatever reason. The killing of them federal agents was on every news channel in America. The case went from local to national. Still no mention of J-Mills name yet which was a good thing. Yet he knew he wasn't out of the clear. Every newspaper that came on the tier talking about that case he would read. He didn't know this old head who Mir was messing with. The whole time he thought he was dealing with Anwar. Being as though Mir folded he was happy he hadn't been. Still the ideal had him vexed because he now knew that Mir was on some other stuff and he assumed that all this extended from dealing with old head. He had no idea that they had been on him.

The newspaper was giving graphic details. Names and faces, who was connected to who, what they had got caught with, etc..... To the best of J-Mills knowledge the old head didn't know anything about him. J-Mills figured all Mir had to do was not mention him and he'll be good. Before all of this he would of bet the bank Mir would of held water, now he just prayed.

J-Mills called Isha's mom house. Her mother picked up crying hysterically. He could barely understand her words. Once he heard her say that Isha had gotten killed he broke down. It felt like somebody squeezed his heart. When he got off the phone he had tears in his eyes. Guys knew he was going through drama because they all knew about the case his dudes had caught but they had no idea of the news he had just heard.

As he walked to his cell everyone moved out of his way. He looked like he might black out. He went in the cell sat on his bonk and staired at the floor. A tear flowed down his face. This was the first time he shed a tear in two decades and he was only twenty

185

two. The death of his lady and unborn child had him stressed out. He couldn't help but to think that somehow because she was dealing with him her death was his fault. He sat there looking at a picture of Isha in a red dress with her hands on her pregnant belly smiling as she posed.

He didn't try to attend her funeral. He knew they wouldn't allow him because she wasn't considered immediate family. He really didn't want to go shackled seeing her laying in a casket. He wanted his last memories to be of her alive.

****

"What's up baby," Angie asked?

Her and the baby came up that Wednesday as usual. What J-Mills was going through had started to show. He had fell into a state of depression and didn't know it. He wasn't working out, eating as often as he usually did or getting his hair cut every week how he used to.

Angie deserved an Oscar for her acting. She knew exactly what was wrong. She expected him to be stressed and depressed. He went on telling her about Isha as if she didn't already know what happened. She could feel in his voice that he was really hurt but she figured with time and her love he'll get over it.

"I'm sorry to hear that Jamil. Me and the baby will always be here for you no matter what," she said trying to let him know that all wasn't lost.

"I know," he sadly said.

Angie was loving the fact that Isha was no longer in the picture. He was vulnerable and in prison where dudes needed love the most at. To her he was like clay in her hands, with the love she planned on showing him she was going to mold him into the man she needed him to be. She left that visit feeling good that everything was going her way.

CHAPTER 46

Over the next couple months of J-Mills bid Angie held that number one spot down. She made every visit and flooded him with pictures of her and their baby giving him a constant reminder of the family he had waiting for him out there.

Even though he still wasn't over the fact Isha was dead he had to pull himself out of the depressed state he was in. He had lost weight and was feeling and looking weak. He had bounced back with ease. He knew he had a lot of work to do when he got to them streets. He was a leader and leaders couldn't afford to break down like regular humans. They have to find solutions that get the job done.

All them thoughts he had of falling back from the game and starting a family was over now. Everything he had worked to build out there had fell apart. His squad was dismantled and he was about to be released soon. The only plus was that he still had money and connects.

On the day J-Mills was going home he woke up bright and early, brushed his teeth and washed his face. He had only gotten four hours of sleep. Him and his dudes were up all night talking. He was putting the plays together for when they came home. They had woke up early in the morning too just to show him some love before he left.

"Jamil Abdullah bag and baggage," the C.O. yelled on the tier. Embracing his dudes one last time before he left, he let them know that he had them when he got to the other side. J-Mills was that kind of dude, when he gave his word he stood on it. If you was affiliated with him you was always taken care of. He saluted all his other dudes from all over on his way out.

J-Mills had butterflies in his stomach as he was getting processed. This was his first bid. Even though it was only a year he still felt strange about to go back into the world. He walked out of the door and from a distance he could see Angie waiting on the outside of her car. When she saw him she began smiling and so did he.

"Mr. Abdullah," this white guy who seem to have come out of nowhere asked? It was two of them in black suits and ties. They was waiting for him, they knew today was his release date. He had tunnel vision when he first came out, all he could see was Angie. He didn't have any detainers but it was no doubt in his mind who they were. His whole mode changed from happy to depressed. He hoped it was a nightmare but knew that it was as real as it gets. Both of them stood there like Agent Smith from the Matrix.

He gave them a look that asked what did they want. Then he looked down and seen some papers in one of their hands. On top was his mugshot. His fear was now a reality.

"You're under arrest for drug conspiracy."

They handcuffed him and started reading him his memorandum rights. Afterwards they put him in the back of their unmarked car. Angie was outside of the gate trying to find out what was going on. The gate opened and the unmarked car slowly rode by. She couldn't see J-Mills through the tinted windows. He could clearly see the worry on her face though.

They took him over Philly to that federal building and tried to interrogate him. Played the good cop bad cop game but seen it wasn't working so they came at him straight. That's when he found out Mir was really snitching. He been heard it but to hear it from the feds hit different. If it wasn't already out there he probably would have never believed them. He would of thought that it was part of the tactics they be using but Mir snitching had already gotten Reef killed and a lot of others locked up.

"Mr. Abdullah look, you been in here for two hours looking at us like we're crazy not saying anything. I suggest you give us something if you ever want to see that pretty little lady again who was waiting for you."

The agent was giving him the rundown of how they had everything they needed to put him away. In front of J-Mills on the table were pictures of dudes that was caught in that indictment and guys who they were still investigating. Their scare tactics were running out. J-Mills wasn't nervous one bit. Death, and going to prison for a long time or life was something he came to terms with and accepted. His whole squad was supposed to have accepted it that's why Mir breaking was a big disappointment.

"I'm a real gangsta. I aint telling ya'll shit. Do what you gotta do but I want ma lawyers," he said nonchalantly.

After he asked for his lawyer they stop questioning him. They were stuck looking stupid as they watched the words come out of his mouth. They weren't used to his type, the were used to turning men into mice and watching them squeal.

"Tough guy huh. You'll change your mind. I seen guys like you come through here then after only a year in prison beg to come back on that 501k. Ready to set their best friends up to get some time off, or you could just rot in prison like John Gotti gangsta. Let's go Stan, we got a true gangsta here." The federal agent face was apple red. He collected the pictures off the table before they left the room. "You can kiss your little lady goodbye. You won't be getting any of that again. Bout time you get out you won't be able to get it up. Don't worry, I like dark meat. I think I'ma go do the kissing for you," the agent said with a little laugh.

The whole time J-Mills gave him a blank stare. Nothing the agent said phased him. He buckled up, he knew he was about to take a long ride. Being locked up and knowing you was about to go away for a long time was a feeling that couldn't be described. With no control over one's life one could become depressed or could stand tall and hold his head up. J-Mills attitude was fuck it. He wasn't about to turn bitch now.

****

Whoever said Muslims and Jews couldn't get along was a lie. When Anwar found out the feds had snatched J-Mills up he sent him one of the best lawyers the country had to offer. Whether it was to make sure J-Mills had adequate representation or it was to make sure he didn't say his name. Whatever it was J-Mills didn't mind. He found out who the lawyer was and knew Anwar was paying big money for him. J-Mills had his own lawyer but chose to go with the one Anwar sent because he was a federal lawyer, not to mention his resumé was way better. He had a stellar reputation for beating the feds, mostly mob cases.

He was a humble tall Jewish older guy who had flown in from California. Everything about him said money, he was filthy rich. He had an aura of someone who ran America from behind the scenes. The first thing he said after introducing himself was, "Don't worry, you're in good hands."

The lawyer laid the paperwork out for J-Mills and they went over everything. He confirmed that Mir was telling. Surprisingly, he was the only one from the people who had gotten locked up which hurt J-Mills even more. He had to come to the realization that you never really know dudes. Dudes talk that real talk but the truth is that situations make or break dudes and Mir let it break him.

191

J-Mills was being housed at the Federal Detention Center in Philly. Angie came to visit him faithfully. J-Mills didn't have plans on going to trail. He heard less than two percent of people who went to trail with the feds won. All the dudes he knew personally who went and lost had gotten thirty to life. He wasn't trying to take that chance with Mir testifying. He knew too much but as of yet he didn't tell them anything about the bodies. Probably because they would burn him too.

The prosecutor started off coming at him with thirty years. After is lawyer worked his magic the prosecutor had came down to one hundred and twenty months. The lawyer didn't advise J-Mills to take it but he did let him know that it was a good deal. Everybody else was taking pleas. After being locked up almost two years that ten years was tempting. He was really considering it. Getting the kind of money he was getting, to only have to pay ten years was nothing. He had until Monday to think about it.

CHAPTER 47

Friday morning was freezing cold pouring down raining outside. Mir's mom had parked her car in the parking lot of Ferry Station Speed Line. She worked in Philly, she always took the train because it was cheaper and faster. Exiting her car she opened her umbrella up and started walking. A masked man ran up on her and put a gun to her face. She started to scream, he started punching her. She went to the ground and kicked her in her face and she went to sleep. He drug her to his car and took her home. On the ride he drove with his mask off. When they arrived at her house he put it back on. She woke up to a hand covering her mouth and a gun to her face.

"Look, you home. We going in here so act regular. I'm telling you If you try anything funny I won't hesitate to kill you, got it?"

She shook her head yeah out of fear.

"If you cooperate aint nothing to worry about. You going to live, trust me."

She shook her head yeah again. It was almost 5:30am. No one was on the street, especially her block. He got her out of the car and rushed her up the steps and into the house. The whole time he held the gun pointed in her back. She was so nervous she fumbled through the keys trying to find the right one to put in the doorknob.

"Give me that shit," the mask man said irritated.

He snatched the keys out of her hand and opened the door. When they got in he tied her hands and legs up and sat her on the couch.

"Please don't rape me, it's money in my dresser," she said as he tied her up.

"Bitch, I don't want none of that old ass pussy. This aint about no money either. You think ya son could tell on all these people and everything going to be good? Nah, it don't work like that. Now what time does his punk ass call?"

"Around 8:00pm."

After hearing that he knew he was going to be there all day but he was prepared to go all the way. He made her call out of work sick. He helped himself to some of the snacks in the cabinets. He didn't care if his fingerprints or DNA was getting all over because he had plans on banging out with the cops like Reef did. He went upstairs to the bathroom and took a piss, took his mask off for a second and looked in the mirror. The reason he kept his mask on was because Mir's mom knew him. Pooh put back on his mask and went back downstairs. All day he starved her, only giving her water, no matter how many times she asked for something to eat. When she had to go to the bathroom he watched her like a C.O. watching an inmate take a urine test. She couldn't answer any of her phone calls except the one that came around 8:00 O'clock.

Like clockwork Mir had called on time. Pooh pick up the phone and heard the operator. He pushed five to accept the call.

"Hey mom," Mir said.

"Sorry to tell you but this aint her," Pooh said disguising his voice making it much deeper so Mir couldn't recognize it.

"Who the fuck is this?"

"Ya worse nightmare."

"Stop playing, put ma mom on the phone."

"You think getting dudes all that time in prison is a game? You got it fucked up."

Mir got quiet, he realized that whoever that was wasn't playing. They really had his mom.

"Listen, if you don't recant everything and set ma dudes free ya mom going to die. It's that simple. I'm taking her for insurance. You won't see her until I see ma dudes. That's the only way she'll survive. Call the prosecutors and do what you got to do. If by any chance you don't follow through she going to pay with her life."

The whole time Mir's mom was crying. Pooh put the phone to her ear and said, "tell this mothafucka something."

"Please do whatever he want baby, please."

"You got that, if you love her you better listen."

Pooh hung up, duct taped and blind folded Mir's mom then took her to a stash house right in the hood and put her in the basement.

****

On the other side of the phone Mir was destroyed. He couldn't believe that he had his mom in this situation. He didn't think about the consequences of his actions because he was too selfish trying to save his own ass. He didn't know what to do when the phone hung up. He tried calling back but no one answered. In his heart he knew it was real. J-Mills came to mind when he thought about who could have this done. He knew how he played, it was no doubt in his mind that this was his work.

That night Mir couldn't sleep. The next day he called his lawyer and told him he wanted to recant everything. His lawyer tried to talk him out of it but he let him know that his mother's life depended on it. He told his lawyer a little about the situation. His lawyer did all the paperwork then got in touch with the prosecutor and J-Mill's lawyer.

J-Mill's lawyer got the good news and took it straight to J-Mills. It came through in the nick of time because J-Mills had set his mind on taking that plea. His lawyer assured him that without Mir's testimony that there was no way they could hold him. His lawyer said he was going to put in a motion to suppress the evidence.

When the prosecutor who was working the case got wind of this she was furious. She paid Mir a visit and threatened to put all the time he was facing back on the table. He didn't break this time, his mom was more important. The prosecutor wanted an explanation of why all of a sudden the change of heart. He told her that he had been lying but she didn't believe him.

The court date for the suppression of evidence motion was set for February 23 about a month away. Pooh still had Mir's mom down the basement. He was treating her terribly. He started feeding her, he needed her alive. Still every time she went to the bathroom he was on her like flies on shit. She was his get out of jail free card, he wanted to make sure she didn't try any desperate moves.

A few days of not going to work or picking up her phone had Mir's mom family and friends concerned. Her sister went to her house only to find no one there. She called the police and filed a missing person report. When the prosecutor found out it was Mir's mom she paid him another visit. She knew him changing his mind had everything to do with his mother's disappearance.

At this time Mir was in Camden County P.C.. A c.o. called him off the block and sent him upstairs so nobody could see him talking to the prosecutor. Mir went from a flamboyant upbeat arrogant person to a humble snitch who wished he could just bury himself until this was all over with. He was tired of coming off the tier and having people look at him how they did. Even the c.o.'s looked at him in disgust.

"Amir Anderson I'm sorry to hear about your mother, I know that's why your trying to back out of your statements. I have the whole city under siege looking for her. We will find her but if you back out they'll win."

"You don't understand, if I don't they'll kill her and I won't be able to live with that."

"Do you know or have any ideal who it is?"

"No but I know the kind of people I'm dealing with. I know they will do it."

The prosecutor didn't care about his mother's wellbeing, all she cared about was her conviction rates. She kept trying to convince him to go through with everything but it was no use. She left disappointed.

****

Drug kingpin turned informant mother comes up missing. That was the headlines of the Courier Post News Paper. One of the dudes who was from Camden who was on the tier with J-Mills had brung him the newspaper. J-Mills laid on the bottom bunk reading it with a smile on his face. He knew it had to be Pooh. The reporters had turned it into a big story. Even though Camden was one of the worse cities in the nation because of politics the city did everything in its power to downplay the crime but not this time.

Mir wasn't saying anything, they didn't know the first place to look but the city was on fire. The D.A. came questioning everybody involved in the case. J-Mills was the only one who didn't take a plea yet and Pooh was the only one not locked up. Maria Austin was the prosecutor who came to see J-Mills. She tried to go at him hard.

J-Mills was taken from the federal detention center in Philly to the prosecutor building in Camden for interrogation. First the prosecutor tried to be nice by offering him cigarettes and coffee. None of which he indulged in but to take advantage of their kindness and play their game he requested a Black and Mild. One was promptly brung to him. He champed it and smoked it while saying he don't know to all of their questions. The prosecutor had got tired of his smart attitude and threatened to take the plea off the table. She was saying everything to call his bluff but J-Mills was unaffected. The tables had turned, he was up on the score board and was trying to win. Prosecutor Maria realized that she was wasting her time and had him taken back over Philly.

****

J-Mills court date had come and he was in the bullpen when his lawyer called him out to talk to him.

"Mr. Abdullah I don't know how things are going to go today but if Mr. Anderson come in here and do what he's supposed to you'll be a free man soon."

That's all J-Mills needed to hear to make his day. When he went in the courtroom he saw Angie sitting in the front row with the baby. He gave her a smile. The only evidence to suppress was Mir's statement against him. Mir came out and took the stand. After swearing on the bible the prosecutor begin questioning him.

"Amir Anderson is it true that you told me that you and the defendant ran a drug operation out of the Parkside section of Camden New Jersey?"

"No, I don't recall telling you that. I do a lot of pills and they be having ma brain fried."

"You mean you're trying to change your story because your mother got kidnapped?"

The prosecutor felt like if he was going to change his story then she was going to make it hard for him.

"No, now that I'm not on drugs and my head is clear I don't think innocent people should be sent to prison because of a lie."

"I don't believe anything you're saying. If he was so innocent then why bring him in this in the first place?"

Questions like this went on for an hour, then it was J-Mill's lawyer turn. J-Mill's lawyer had Mir on the stand crying talking about how he was coerced into implementing J-Mills and Pooh because the feds were after them. When Goldstein rested his case the judge decided not to take the case to trial since the only witness said he didn't have anything to do with it. Judge Thornton dismissed the case and J-Mills was able to go free that same day.

J-Mills got up shook his lawyer's hand, turned to Angie and seen that she was in happy tears. He hugged and kissed her and the baby. He had to go back to the federal detention center until he was properly processed out.

****

Later that day he was released. Angie was outside waiting. He never was happier to see her more than now. He palmed her ass while tonguing her down. His mother was at Angie's house watching their son. When he went in the house his son ran in his arms yelling, "daddy, daddy's home." J-Mills picked him up. It was one of the best feeling ever.

****

Once Pooh found out J-Mills case had gotten dismissed he knew he was in the clear. Even though he was still on the run and planed on staying on the run until they caught him. He waited late that night around three something in the morning and put Mir's mom in the trunk of a car. That time of the morning the streets were empty, but Pooh knew the feds was still Lurking. He pulled over on the ten hundred block of Empire near the truck stop. He took her out of the truck and sat her on the side of the street still tied up and blind folded.

"I told you I was going to release you if ya son held up his end. He did so you good. Just wait five minutes," Pooh said and jumped in his wheels and left. He still had no plans on getting up with J-Mills, not yet anyway. He knew J-Mills was probably being watched.

Print Name:

Address:

City: State: Zip:

Phone:

Mail to: Parkside Entertainment LLC

PO Box 2176

Clementon, NJ 08021

Contact Info: Instagram @TyeMease

Parksideentertainmentllc.com

Name	Quantity	Date	Price
Gucci Girls			
Poetic Kisses			
Grand Rising			

Acknowledgements

Thanks to the people. I get a lot of support when I'm out and I really wanted to let people know that I'm grateful and humbled. The feedback I get be great. It inspires me to go harder and really enjoy the process. I really learnt to love being out and about pushing my book. It's not the easiest thing but it's a pleasure that can't be describe. Just knowing people embrace my talent means a lot to me. Forever grateful.

Sincerely, Tyrone Mease

www.ingramcontent.com/pod-product-compliance
Lightning Source LLC
Chambersburg PA
CBHW070702280626
47159CB00022B/1793